4-10-09

Hinton   c.1
The order of things

THE ORDER *of* THINGS

Also by Lynne Hinton

THE
ORDER
OF THINGS

Lynne Hinton

ST. MARTIN'S PRESS · NEW YORK

This is a work of fiction. All of the characters, organizations, and events portrayed in this novel are either products of the author's imagination or are used fictitiously.

www.stmartins.com

Book design by Mary A. Wirth

LIBRARY OF CONGRESS CATALOGING-IN-PUBLICATION DATA

Hinton, J. Lynne.
    The order of things / Lynne Hinton.—1st ed.
        p. cm.
    ISBN-13: 978-0-312-34796-3
    ISBN-10: 0-312-34796-0
  1. Women librarians—Fiction. 2. Prisoners—Fiction.
3. Friendship—Fiction. I. Title.

    PS3558.I457073   2009
    813'.54—dc22

                                            2008035782

First Edition: March 2009

10 9 8 7 6 5 4 3 2 1

For librarians everywhere.
Thanks for keeping the order.
And for Ronnie Sykes,
genius, artist, friend.

CONTENTS

ACKNOWLEDGMENTS

I gratefully acknowledge the editorial staff at St. Martin's Press, especially Kylah McNeill. Thank you for your many acts of kindness! Thank you also to Nichole Argyres and Frances Sayers.

As always, I am grateful to my agent, Sally McMillan. I'd be lost without you.

Finally, to my husband, Bob, thank you for more than twenty years of encouragement, support, and chocolate marshmallows. I am the luckiest woman in the world!

THE ORDER *of* THINGS

ONE

362.21

ℳENTAL ILLNESS

I lost and found the order of things the year the butterflies didn't migrate down from the mountains. Low sky and hot, it was a parched summer, and the days dragged on like the smell of smoke after a fire.

The weatherman on Channel 10 claimed that the absence of the butterflies had to do with the virus that killed the carpenter bees the year before; that it had spread to the larvae of other insects or settled upon the milkweed that the winged creatures ingested. But I think it was just the heat.

I think the heavy wet air hung like a thick curtain, stretching from the foothills to the sand hills, a barricade of weather, and would not open for swallowtails or skippers, monarchs or sulphurs, or the faint whisper of hope that might have saved me from my decline.

To a casual observer, butterflies appear wispy and undetermined, but really they are just as hardworking as the hummingbird or the dirt dauber. They glide maybe instead of dart, like the dragonfly and mosquito, but they are not idle. They understand that they have places to go. They stretch out those long curved bit of wings as if they enjoy showing off for the wind and the eye of the beholder, but they always realize their destination. They flap and hover, sometimes going more than seventy miles a day.

I've seen streaks of magenta on a butterfly that would make my eyes burn, small smooth spots of black dancing upon yellow wings, and I have been dazed by the sleepy parachuting way they float. But I know better than to be fooled by a butterfly; she's more than just a pretty face. She is engineered to be efficient and beautiful.

They burst forth from egg to caterpillar and eat as quickly and as much as they can digest, growing as large as is possible while shedding several layers of skin. Then they make themselves a hollow place to lie, a safe and protected chrysalis where they wait patiently for the spinning and changing of the caterpillars with which they began. And after a death of what is hard and tight and miserable, they fight their way through webs of silk and dust, a tangle of what they used to be, emerging as something different, something extraordinary, to set sail to the sight of endless sun.

The North American butterflies start their descent to Mexico from roosts high in bat caves and along ridges of green hills thousands of miles away. Gliding toward the cool mountains, they are met with predators, pesticides, and fatigue. But millions of butterflies manage a migration and millions make it back. They are brawny and plucky and they will not light in a place or season that is unwelcoming.

I knew then, when the earth turned brown and the air stifled any pleasure from the coming together and breaking apart of clouds, when the warmth rose and swelled like tides in the sea, that heat was holding back my resolve and forcing the detour of the bright and brilliant insects upon which, for me, summer is marked. Without much of a fight, I sank into the place I had fought to hide and felt no remorse or sadness at my loss, only a tinge of disappointment that I had missed the butterflies.

Once fallen, however, I decided in the days of reflection of that colorless season, that if it must be done, summer is a good arrangement of days in which to lose oneself. Not because the Earth with its revolutions and its increased daylight is as welcoming of it as it is in the opposite season, but rather because you're rarely noticed and thereby given a reprieve from cheerful well-meaning friends who call you or drop by just to make sure you've haven't bought a gun or hoarded medications. Most people assume you're on some extended vacation or appear absentminded only because you're inclined toward leisure. Everybody's out of touch anyway, so days can pass and no one even misses you; they just figure you're hiking at the state park or that you took a day trip to the coast.

From Memorial Day to Labor Day, May to September, people seem to put their anxious caregiving on hold, their temptations to worry stored away for winter, while supposing that distant friends and family members are enjoying the long sun and the invitation to go outside. They couldn't possibly imagine that anybody they know could be strangled by darkness in such a fair time as this.

In the colder seasons it's different because, unlike in summer, everybody suffers some depression in the winter. It's just a common reaction to gray days and unfulfilled holidays. We're sympathetic with the mentally ill during that frozen time because everybody understands how sadness might win out in the hours of darkness.

This sense of despondency was not my first experience of falling away from myself. It has happened to me before, and since it does not always fall upon my spirit in one particular period of time, I cannot claim to have some seasonal disorder or light sensitivity. I guess one would say that I am simply prone to this kind of thing. Like Mama and her gout or Jane Mackay, one of the other librarians, and her cold sores, I just have a bent toward the shadows.

Usually, the sorrow is manageable. I move through it the way a person moves through a sprained joint or pulled muscle. I simply find another way to step or climb. It hurts, smarts really, but it's something that can be done. I just try and put the sadness aside, shelve it like a book no longer useful. I know it's there. It slows me down, but I just choose not to let it stop me. Most of the time that system works. A couple of times it has not.

I lost myself the first time when I was only four. I do not recall exactly what happened or how I coped. I only remember feeling very small, arms and legs pulled inside myself, a turtle in its shell, and being passed from one adult's lap to another, from one set of arms to a broad chest, slung across a hip and thrown across a back. It was as if I were an infant or a sack of wheat.

My mother says I stopped participating in life, arrested the progress, just after I learned to speak, something that already arrived very late in my development, and she always thought my fall into despondency was because I was afraid of the power of words. She told me once that when I was a child I had never seemed comfortable in conversation, that the nature of my play had always been quiet. She claimed that it concerned her at first, especially when I was silent for so long and then so completely after saying my first words, but that later she simply accepted that I would talk when it was necessary. She decided not to see it as a disability and not to pull me into meaningless speech just to assuage her fears.

I cannot say if she was right about the cause of the early fit of sadness, but I do remember thinking that hearing the sound of my own voice was frightening in a way that paralyzed me. Once I heard the sounds of words coming from my lips and recognized the power of being understood by others, it was as if I suddenly knew I was, because of the privilege of communication, somehow different from everything else in creation. The words I spoke, the ways I could name and organize my thoughts, suddenly set me apart from the trees and the river, insects and birds, the animals to which I had always felt connected. Once I heard them, felt the sounds being created from the combination of my tongue and brain, the power of such a thing saddened me.

I did not want to speak because somehow I believed it changed the very nature of who I was in the world. The thought of being separate simply weighted me down and bottled me up. I did not like, nor did I want to own, my voice.

I stayed that way, wrapped into myself, for months and I do not recall what finally loosened the words, stretched my limbs, or settled my spirit. I just know that somehow a conversation began with my mother, something about a neighbor, a man who died alone in a fishing boat far in the middle of the ocean. Since she had never stopped talking to me, just abstained from trying to pull me in the discussion, she brought the news of the man's death the way she reported all of the day's events to me. And somehow, I just recall being struck by how alone he was when he died. I asked a question—I don't even know what it was—and heard an answer. My mother didn't seem to be alarmed or relieved at hearing my voice, just continued in the conversation. And afterward, I did not need to be carried any longer.

There was another time of silence and sadness tangled together in my life that I remember. I became disordered and lost when I was sixteen and had been recently pregnant. I miscarried at seven months in the autumn season and I simply fell away from myself again. Unlike the first time, however, my adolescent descent didn't come quick and furious. My spirit was not suddenly lifeless like my distended womb. I did not suddenly feel frozen and still and small, broken by the disappointment of being separate. This loss felt more like a slow pulling of threads, like a tear in fabric, a loosening and widening along the sharp edges of my mind. Just like this time, this last time, at sixteen I hardly even noticed as it happened.

Once all the pieces had finally come undone and I was not able to carry on my usual responsibilities, I was taken out of school, kept at home. I didn't go to a doctor or a counselor. Mama didn't have the money or the insurance to cover such a thing. And I figure no one intervened, no one came to the house to try and pull me out or away from my loss, because they all just assumed it was because of the baby and its dying inside me, the sorrow of motherhood and adolescence knotting up. I think they expected that I'd soon snap out of it, so they just left me alone.

I misspent about a year that time; try as I may, I cannot recall one major event from any of those months as I lay in my bed coloring pictures in children's coloring books. Not Christmas or birthdays, mine or my mother's, or New Year's Eve. I do not remember wide shoulders or fleshy arms or being held or wrapped. That event of brokenness is managed in my memory only by a series of manila pages with pictures of oversized bears and frogs, elephants and fairies, a collage of big smiling fantasies lumbering from drawing to drawing.

My mother, not knowing what else to do for me, not able to lift me and walk with me slung about her hip, bought new coloring books from the dime store every week. "Here you go, babe," she'd say, placing them near my head on the pillow, and I filled them up and threw them away. I drew until the sticks of wax were pounded down to mere stubs of deep clear color, until every page was filled in, every picture painted.

Attentive as a nurse, Mama would come into the room, lean across my bed, and wipe off the shards of crayons and the tiny pieces of paper that clung to my blanket and the heel of my hand.

"I found a book with fairies and angels," she said one day, having spent her lunch hour in dime stores downtown, trying to find something, anything, that might lift me away from the sadness.

She bought box after box of crayons, book after book of nursery rhymes and storybook pictures, and she would hand them to me with a reassuring hand and a tense shaky smile. And this is the way it went month after month. It became a satisfactory life.

Then finally one day—a Thursday, I remember—I got out of the bed, went to my closet, and pulled out a yellow dress, put it on with my hiking boots, and walked to school. No one was more surprised than I since I had made no plans to recover. But something about the angle of light from the morning sun, the little wax flakes of yellow and green spread all around me, and my mother's steady chin, lifted me out of my despair and ushered me back into the world.

I was thirty-five-pounds lighter, fingertips stained with primary colors, and more than two semesters behind, but it didn't take long before I gained weight, returned to my natural pigmentation, caught up with the other students, and graduated on time. And as I reflect upon my teenage misfortune, I realize it unfolded and stretched away in a manner that is similar to my early childhood event, I still don't know exactly how it happened or how I overcame it.

This last time, the summer time, the time the butterflies stayed away, I was not distracted by pregnancy or the loss of a baby. I was not fretful about being a single mother or missing my senior year of school. I was not suddenly frightened by the sound of my voice or the strength of my words, I simply felt bits and pieces of myself fall aside, like the layers of clothes I shed with the coming of such a hot season.

The symptoms at age thirty-three were slow to show themselves. I, along with those who know me best, went weeks without realizing anything was wrong. At first, it was as simple as losing my sense of direction. I couldn't remember which way I was going. I couldn't place a location in my mind or get a clear picture of a park or building that everyone knew I had been to a million times. I would hear a name or be driving somewhere and suddenly feel as if I were in a town I had never been in, a life that was nothing like mine.

"You okay?" the security guard asked me once as I stood at the edge of the parking lot trying to recall the color and make of the car I was driving. I felt him watch me closely.

"Do you know who I am?" I asked, not quite sure what I expected to hear.

"You work at the library," he answered. "I don't think I've ever learned your name," he added.

I nodded. "And my car," I noted, "do you know my car?"

He scratched his head and considered the question.

"Blue Toyota," he replied. "An old one, muffler is a bit too loud."

And then, without hesitation or judgment, he nodded in the direction where I had parked just eight hours earlier. "Third row, about halfway down." He paused. "It happens a lot," he said, smiling.

But I knew it didn't happen a lot with me. And I began to notice soon that after forgetting directions and the make of my car, I forgot places and events, tiny pieces of information I had long carried in my mind, I quit caring about things, like knowing where I was, being worried that I was lost, or even the basics like if I brushed my hair or matched my earrings. I didn't care if I talked too loud or answered a person's questions. I wasn't concerned if I ate dinner or if I watered the African violets that lined the windowsill in my upstairs bathroom. It didn't matter if I kept my appointments or changed the litter in the cat box. And then eventually, I didn't even care if I ever left my bed.

May unfolded into June. The seniors graduated. The freshmen matriculated. The sophomores and juniors went on international study tours. The professors went on their exotic summer vacations. The cafeteria and fitness center slowed. The campus fell quiet and I just wanted to sleep.

Beginning around the middle of the month of June, a few people, coworkers at the library, my mother, a neighbor— Mrs. Bishop, who watched me through her kitchen window—did begin to show signs that they suspected that something was not quite right with me. There were an increased number of phone calls from Mama and a few unexpected visits from my attentive neighbor. And yet, for weeks, even though I appeared disheveled and bore no signs of a physical ailment, I managed to convince them I had a virus or was tired from the heat, and for the beginning weeks of that long, hot summer, they mostly left me alone.

At work, however, when it soon got around that I was not taking vacation time or had discovered some new summer sport that kept me distracted, when it was common knowledge that I wasn't sick with cancer or some other horrible disease, a few of the other staff started to wonder where I was and what I was doing. Having always been a very dedicated and hardworking reference librarian on the university campus, one about whom the others had never complained, it took a while, but not that long, before my colleagues were tired of picking up my slack.

After a number of grievances, the director of library services at the school, my boss, Charles Hyde, Charlie, looked at me with a keen eye, watching me in the mornings when I got out of my car, at my desk when I answered the phones, when I walked into the stacks and returned the books that were left on the table. He didn't say anything for the longest time, but after Mary Simpson, the library manager, threatened to quit if he didn't do something about his reference librarian who was no longer doing her job, he waited until late in the afternoon on a Wednesday and called me to his office.

I had a bit of time to prepare myself because Jane told me that I had been reported. She walked over to my desk that morning after I had arrived a couple of hours late, fingers covering her mouth as she tried to hide her cold sore, and told me.

"Mary's turned you in," she said, her voice just above a whisper. She glanced around to see if anyone was watching. She dropped her hand away from her lips. "She said that you're taking advantage of the library." Jane paused, glancing around again. "She said you're taking advantage of Mr. Hyde. What are you going to do?" she asked.

I shrugged. "I guess I'll do whatever I have to do," I replied.

Jane nodded and slipped away, her face to the floor.

Charlie called me for a meeting later that afternoon. I walked in and he shut the door so nobody else would hear and pulled out the chair for me from behind the file cabinet. I slumped into it. As he headed around to his desk, I could feel his concern, the awkwardness he felt in having to reprimand me. I knew he didn't like doing what he was about to do.

Charlie didn't like conflict and he rarely interfered in the lives of his personnel. He said to every person he hired, "You don't need to tell me everything about what is going on in your life. If you need a day off or need to be at home, just work it out with the other librarians and do what you need to do. As long as the job gets done, I'm satisfied."

And that was the way of things in the library. We never bothered him about dentist visits or sick children. We found people to fill in when we needed to be away. We managed our personal lives with one another, without drama or fanfare, and for the most part, there were very few problems.

It all changed, however, during that summer. The butter-flies were missing and the heat was oppressive and I had tampered with the system. Folks were getting tired of it. Jane and Mary were tired of covering for me. Charlie was forced to become involved. For the director of library serv-ices at the university, this was not a pleasurable thing.

He sat at his desk, sliding his hands through his curly brown hair, a nervous habit I had only seen during budget time and when he had to fire the janitor after finding him drunk and naked sitting in the history section of the library, reading the story of a village in France that was bombed dur-ing the war. The old man was weeping and singing verses of French songs, a bottle of red wine tucked under his arm. No one even knew the man who swept the floors and emptied our trash was European and certainly no one expected him to show up to work during parents' week disrobed and homesick for France. It was sad for everyone and a little frightening for the freshman U.S. history class whose mem-bers had been released from class to go to the library and re-search their midterm papers. Once the incident was reported to the president of the university, there was no alternative, Charlie had to let him go.

He sat up in his chair and then back. He nodded his head as if he were conversing with someone else. He took a deep breath. I simply waited for him to begin.

"A librarian must have use of all her faculties," Charlie finally said, blowing out a long breath. And then he tapped his left and right forefingers on the edge of his desk as if he were playing the piano. He cleared his throat and glanced up at me with this kind of helpless expression, as if he needed some encouragement that he had done the right thing.

I searched his eyes and recognized the look of my mother's worry. It is, after all, memorized deep in my psyche. Once I saw that, I knew what had to be done. And so without a response, without saying a word of agreement or discontent, I leaned over and picked up the receiver on the phone by his right elbow and dialed the infirmary.

Charlie pulled away from the desk and turned his chair to face the window while I made the appointment, a small but genuine show of respect. It was as if I were changing clothes or handling my checkbook. He cast his eyes away and it was so small and so kind an action I found myself touched by his tenderness. I received a date and time to see the doctor and I simply hung up the phone and walked out of his office without Charlie saying anything else.

I noticed Mary Simpson standing near the corridor that led to Charlie's office. She smiled sympathetically and I returned the greeting. After all, I felt no ill will toward her for turning me in. With a daughter on drugs and a mother in the nursing home, she had problems of her own. She didn't need to be pulling my load in the library. She was right to report me and I knew it.

I returned to the reference section and started reshelving the encyclopedias. Charlie came out of his office, spoke briefly to his manager, probably explaining that the problem had been solved, and walked over to my section. He helped me put up the large atlas that somebody had taken from the map drawer. His arm rubbed slightly against mine as he took my end from me so that he could place it on the rack. And then Charlie turned to me and nodded as if I had done the right thing. After that, he walked over to the checkout counter and began loading books on the cart. Getting intervention was just that simple.

My appointment at the infirmary was the next day. With the academic school year ended and summer school between sessions, there were not that many patients needing to be seen. I went during my lunch period so that I wouldn't have to ask Mary or Jane to find someone to replace me at the reference desk. I knew I had reached my limit of grace with the library staff.

Once on my way, however, it took me much longer than I expected, about thirty minutes, to find the infirmary. Still struggling with the loss of my sense of direction, I could no longer find my way around the university campus. All the paths and signs and buildings seemed strangely unfamiliar and confusing. Upon leaving, I had been sure that the clinic was behind the library next to the cafeteria and that the administration building was down a paved road to the right. But I was wrong. The infirmary was beside the personnel office, next to the fitness center, near the center of campus. I had walked past it four times without recognizing it. Because of my loss of orientation within the campus, I was more than a few minutes late.

First, I signed in, and then I waited until the nurse, Mary Joe Driver, who reads everything we have in the library about sexual dysfunction, came to the door and called my name.

There was no one else in the waiting room and I was glad not to have to share the space with students who might recognize me from the library.

Nurse Driver took me to a corner in the hall where she weighed me and took my temperature, my pulse, and the other vitals. Having received my assistance in the library and knowing me professionally, she asked me about work, how things were. And while she talked about the university and how everything had changed, the heat, and the incoming freshman class, I wondered whether indifference could alter the basic human functions that she was testing, if my blood pressure and my heart rate were slowed or quickened by the feelings of discontent, and I couldn't help but wonder if she read the books she checked out for herself or was trying to figure out the problems of somebody else.

I simply answered her questions and participated in the conversation politely. I did not comment about the new president or the new vaccinations required of all students. I nodded and smiled and tried to read the numbers on the thermometer and the scales and the blood pressure monitor. And then she led me to the little examining room to wait for the doctor.

In the small room, there were posters about sexually transmitted diseases and tooth decay and an old wallpaper border that drooped in the corners. The room was painted mauve, a kind of dingy purple. A small tinted window sat high in the wall and was slightly open so that I could hear the outside noises of lawn mowers and people walking past.

I sat and waited for the doctor and thought about all the

hundreds of young college students who had sat on this same table learning the news of infections and pregnancies, the complications of eating disorders and binge drinking. I thought of all of the ways the students figured out how to keep the prognosis from their parents and all of the ways a young person grieves. I thought of all the diseases, all the bad news, all the tests and questions and blood samples and wondered how many people, if any, had come in complaining of feeling lost from themselves.

Dr. Simmons, the college physician, a muddle of a man himself, finally came into the room. I had seen him a few times before. Once when I had strep throat and a couple of times because of migraines. I don't think he remembered me.

He asked me what was wrong as he looked over my chart, humming slightly, and then pulled off his reading glasses and seemed to be studying my face. I told him I thought I was depressed or sad or something that was making me not care about anything. I told him I slept too much and that I was having difficulty remembering directions. He stood over me, nodding and smiling as if he had guessed such a thing, and listened to my heart, took my blood pressure again. He checked my reflexes, shined a tiny bright light into my eyes and asked how long I had been feeling like this. I said a few weeks. And then he sat down on his stool.

He glanced back over my medical history and wanted to know if I had been under a lot of stress in recent months, if anyone I loved had died, or if I had suffered a major breakup. To all of these I responded negatively while he chewed on the end of his pen, squinting his eyes at me, and continued making a humming noise while he jotted a few notes on my chart. Then he was silent. I watched him as he diagnosed me, as he put together all of the information and came up with a reasonable explanation for my sorrow. Finally, he spoke up, clear and confident of his findings.

"Since there is no direct cause for these feelings of discontent," Dr. Simmons said, just after clearing his throat, "you must be experiencing some hormonal surge."

I must have looked surprised. I know I felt surprised since of all of the reasons I had given myself for feeling this way, the monthly discharge I had been experiencing quite regularly for almost twenty years had not been considered.

He closed my chart and continued. "And this surge, just like your cycles, will one day pass." He seemed quite self-assured, smiled at me, and since I have always been a person who honored the authority of physicians, I decided to believe him.

And then, feeling even more confident of his diagnosis, his ability to identify a problem, Dr. Simmons sized me up a few minutes more. I think my smile boosted his confidence. He nodded at me or himself, I'm not sure, and added that I was probably too easily affected by what goes on around me, that I needed a hobby or a friend and that maybe I should even think about a new profession since the library was known to hamper feelings of enthusiasm and spawn a certain amount of listlessness.

He gave me a few samples of sleeping pills, which seemed odd since that was the one activity in which I had not lost interest, patted me on the leg, and wrote a note of reference, sending me to a psychology professor who set up her practice in the storage room behind the campus police office. Nurse Mary Joe Driver called and made me an appointment and I went back to the library feeling no different than I had before I went. I even got lost again, ending up at the science building on the other side of the campus. I eventually made my way back to the library without anyone noticing that I had gone and returned. I had my first meeting with the psychologist the following week.

Dr. Lincoln was a perky young woman, a recent Ph.D. recipient, and I believe she truly thought she could help me. After taking a long history of my life, filling out three or four forms, she took me into her office and had me sit on a sofa. She studied exactly where on the couch I sat, how I crossed my legs, and seemed even to count the number of times I smiled.

After having me explain how I felt by using a number of assessment tools, including a scale from one to ten, with one being, "I want to kill myself," and ten being "I'm as happy as I've ever been," picking the closest to my feelings using a series of pictures of expressive faces, and having me read a book of cartoons while she measured my laughter, she decided that she could use me in her recently funded research project. Dr. Lincoln seemed pleased at the prospects of what I could offer.

During our second visit, she tried to teach me how to hold off what she defined as "the negative emotion" by having me breathe my fears into a bag and surround myself in

some bright color that could shield me from the poison that
she said gets into my psyche. It took a few tries before I got
the hang of exhaling in a bag.

For my color, originally I chose pink, but after having
thoughts of being covered in Pepto-Bismol, I settled on
purple. I surrounded myself in a purple bubble and tried to
let the color protect me. I wanted the purple to work. I
closed my eyes and saw everything in purple.

We met five times and she spent an extra half hour with
me during each of our sessions because she said I was an
interesting subject, a classic model of study for her research.
Dr. Lincoln also informed me during one of our times together that she didn't like her colleagues in the psychology
department, that most of them were just quacks, and that
she was confident that she would one day be famous.

For weeks, throughout the entire month of July, I did all
of her exercises. I closed my eyes and breathed in the bag
and then held it tight and far away. I visualized happiness
as a light all around me, lit up like the sky at dusk. I soaked
in purple, breathed in purple, even dreamed in purple.

I tried her other suggestions. I wrote down affirmations
of my self-worth and taped them on my mirrors. I started
keeping a journal. I exhaled in long, even puffs. I followed
her finger as she sat in front of me and waved it from side
to side, trying to hypnotize me.

I waited for Dr. Lincoln's therapy to bring me back to
myself, to pull the threads together, but somehow, the contents from my bag of pessimism leaked out the top or spilled
through a weak corner or small crack and seeped back into

my lungs. Somehow, the hypnosis didn't eliminate "the negative emotion" and the purple could not save me. And even though I hated to be deemed unsuitable for her research and dropped as her perfect role model, when after more than six weeks she finally asked, I could not confirm that I was any better.

After immediately deciding I no longer fit her needs, Dr. Lincoln sent me to a therapist, a man off-campus but who was employed by the university, who specialized in group work. After an initial assessment, I was assigned to a group of other professionals who were diagnosed with various and assorted mental illnesses. The doctor seemed to think he could offer instruction to "bridge gaps in socialization," as he put it, where one-on-one talk therapy had failed.

In my appointed group, there was a post office employee with an anxiety disorder and a food service worker struggling with obsessive-compulsive disorder, a campus policeman who was just diagnosed with cancer and who had developed a problem with anger management, and a retired professor whose wife had just left him for the Methodist minister in town and who could not stop crying.

We gathered on Tuesday nights and we sat in a circle and signed our names to promises of confidentiality that we wouldn't talk about what happened or who was there. I signed the paper and even though my mother was terribly curious about a man who cried continuously over being left by his wife and had tried a number of ways to learn his name, I never broke the promise.

After our fourth meeting, however, I was invited to leave

the group when I initiated the discussion that since we were all so open with our pitiful stories of trouble and loss, Dr. Marshall, the psychiatrist in charge, the one who specialized in group dynamics and mental illness, should at least let us read the comments he wrote about each one of us after every session.

The postal worker and the grieving professor didn't even realize he was taking notes on them. They had never paid attention to the therapist during our sessions. I, however, had noticed Dr. Marshall from the first meeting as the pages in his little notebook filled and turned while we talked about the dark recesses of our minds. I watched him as he smiled and nodded with each entry, always eager to pull us back to a line of thinking he seemed particularly interested in.

Although I could see that the doctor was angry at me for voicing my observation, I didn't apologize for what I did. I'm a librarian. I notice things. I'm curious. I'm just made that way.

Since I knew the therapist's work, I asked him if he was gathering material for his third, bestselling *How to Get Out of What You've Gotten In* psychology book. The question didn't set well with him or the other group members. The angry policeman stormed out and the chef with obsessive-compulsive disorder began counting spots on the ceiling. The doctor slammed his book closed and it was soon obvious that I was going to be asked to leave.

I was somewhat disappointed that I could not continue in the group process. I found that the revelations of these deeply troubled people actually gave me some focus. I was fascinated in a way with the ease in which some folks tell things to strangers that they swear they have never before said to anyone. The intimacy in the group, the way the clients listened to one another, the cop and the mailman becoming friends, touched me in some deep and profound way. I started to like my fellow group members. I cared about them and wondered how they were doing when we weren't together.

I even found myself feeling a little lighter when I went home after a meeting because there was some brief but clear comfort in knowing that crazy people can appear so normal. We get up, go to our jobs, come home, watch the evening news. We are likely never to be noticed. We look like everybody else. There's no mark on our foreheads or sticker on our cars.

It seems as if those of us fallen away from ourselves, broken or lost, can walk around posing like we never had a bad day, that we're just like everyone else. We cook a great dinner. We laugh at jokes. We pass along the mail or arrest a thief or teach a class or help someone with research and nobody suspects a thing. And yet the truth I learned from that group is that we're only a paint job, one or two light coats trying to cover each other, trying to hide what lies beneath. Everything can appear to be exactly fine until someone rubs it with a little pressure and suddenly the real color starts to bleed through.

After meeting those folks in my group, I shall never be surprised again at the people who confess to mental illness. We are the very ones that no one suspects, the very ones who seem to hold it all together and function perfectly in the world.

IT WAS ABOUT two weeks after being dismissed from Dr. Marshall's group and about three days after hearing the news that the college professor whose wife had left him committed suicide, just nearing the end of summer, just before the new school year was to begin, that it became obvious that the cheap paint splashed over my heart was peeling. I was finding no relief from my problems, no sense of getting closer to myself. What I had tried was not doing the job.

"Are you coming to work?" Charlie called and asked on the Monday I decided to go to the hospital.

"I don't think so," I replied. I didn't know what time of day it was. I didn't know where I was supposed to be.

"Do you want me to send someone over?" he asked.

I considered his offer.

"I don't think anything's worked," I said, although I wasn't sure why I did.

"I know," Charlie responded. "You've got good coverage," he added.

I felt confused.

"Insurance," he explained.

"Right," I said, and suddenly understood what I needed to do.

"You want me to take you?" Charlie asked.

"No, I'll figure that out," I responded, hung up the phone, and called the ambulance.

Talk therapy, one-on-one and in a group, sleeping pills, and a pretense that everything was just fine were not working. I knew I had to find help. The butterflies, gone and unaccounted for, the summer dragging on without reprieve, had taken its toll.

973.099

$\mathscr{P}$RESIDENTS

After the phone call from Charlie, I was taken by ambulance to the local hospital. After a brief examination in the emergency room by a physician and a couple of nurses and my confession of not being able to manage the sadness, it was decided that I should be sent to a psychiatric facility, the one in the neighboring village of Vanceboro. I had not heard of it.

The facility, I soon discovered, was a nice private hospital with cheerful walls and real plants in the hallways and lobby, an outside sitting area for smokers and claustrophobics, and a multipurpose room that served as the gym and scream therapy center. In the emergency department I was given the name of the person I would see and allowed one phone call to ask someone to pick up some things from my place for me. After that, I would be released from the hospital and driven to Vanceboro by ambulance.

I signed a few forms, was given some crackers and a soda, and the nurse waited until my neighbor arrived before having me leave the emergency department. There was a place on the forms for Mrs. Bishop to sign as well. It was more than I expected to have to ask from her, packing my bags, and giving her signature as a witness to my instructions, but once she spoke to the nurse, she didn't seem to mind. She even wanted to ride with me to the psychiatric hospital.

I agreed to let her even though Mama offered to go too. I was allowed to call her as well just before I left the emergency room and I knew it hurt her for me to ask my neighbor, but I didn't want her pulled into my despair. I didn't want her hot breath filling up the space between us. I didn't want her pinching and discarding the balls of lint stuck to my blouse or straining to pretend we were only taking a ride to a movie or to shop. I didn't want the burden of her worry adding to what I already carried.

I knew my neighbor, a widow, understood the long, hard weeks in summer and I knew without asking that she would take care of my cat and the few plants I had not yet killed. I knew she would not judge or smother me and I knew, because of her recent loss of her husband of forty-three years and the disappointment of never having children, she could well understand the ease with which a person can despair. Even though we had not talked a lot to each other, were not very social together, I trusted her. I knew she would not make more of the request than what it was. I knew she would pack what I asked and not put in extra things that were intended to bring a smile or add a bit of pleasure to my stay, but that would instead make me feel pathetic and overwrought.

Once we arrived at the facility, Mrs. Bishop got out quickly from the ambulance, stood by the door, and waited until I got out. Then she closed the door and walked with me and the driver inside the hospital to the front desk. The attendant left us alone in the waiting area while she went behind the locked doors to turn over the information she had received from the nurse at the emergency department. My neighbor sat beside me on the sofa and held on tightly to my hand. When I turned to thank her for being with me I saw the cloudy look in her eyes. A woman stood in the doorway and called my name.

"You will find your way," Mrs. Bishop finally said as she turned me loose.

I nodded and left her sitting in the waiting room. And even though I did not watch, I walked away confident that before she called a taxi and headed out she would arrange the magazines on the coffee table and check the soil in the plants by the door. She was awkward in the setting of a psychiatric hospital, but she understood that there are some things that no matter where they are situated or how she was feeling, still required her attention.

At Holly Pines, I noticed right away, the attendants and nurses wore bright colors and comfortable shoes. The only ways, in fact, that you could tell who was a patient and who was an employee were the thin yellow bands taped around the patients' wrists and the casual familiarity with the surroundings, a somewhat lighter disposition than that displayed by most of the employees. It was obvious that the members of the staff were trying to underscore the commonality of all of us, trying not to make the patients feel any more isolated and alone than most of us already felt. Wearing orange or pink shirts was, I think, a requirement for psychiatric hospital workers.

I was taken to a treatment room and given a physical examination by the charge nurse, Louise, a middle-aged woman with a crew cut and a tattoo of barbed wire wrapped around the middle of her arm. She was kind but firm, taking down the information with a professional coolness and courtesy. She called me by my first name and acted as if my coming to Holly Pines was a typical and usual event for anyone. She did not ask me to explain what I thought was wrong or describe any feelings of despair or concern.

She quickly assessed all my vital signs, made a list of all of the medications I had been on, and offered me decaf coffee or a glass of water. I declined and she put all of the information she had received during the examination, as well as a faxed letter from the hospital emergency room and the documents that came with me, in a three-ring bound notebook. She smiled and then Farrell, an attendant, a nice-looking young man, inspected my suitcase and purse for guns or knives or anything sharp or dangerous, I suppose. I suddenly became worried about what Mrs. Bishop may have packed and considered that maybe I should have asked her for specifics. I wondered if she had added anything extra to my things and if candy bars were considered contraband.

Farrell winked as he went through my belongings and then made a kind of clucking noise, a means of disapproval, as he removed my curling iron and fingernail clippers and placed them in a plastic bag that was left at the front counter. Mrs. Bishop was not at fault for those things. I had asked for them. However, I never cared for Farrell after that. I saw no need for his judgment.

I was immediately given a sedative, dinner on a plastic plate, and shown to my assigned room. It was as if I had just checked into a Holiday Inn, except of course having my personal items confiscated and being locked behind a number of thick doors. I sat a few minutes on my bed, considering all that I had managed that day, getting to the hospital, calling Mrs. Bishop to pack my bags and ride with me to Vanceboro, and felt a certain element of pride at all that I had done. Maybe I was crazy, but I was still able to order the things that needed attention.

I changed into my pajamas, pulled down the sheets and thin bedspread, fluffed the institutional foam pillow, and climbed into bed. Even in a strange place, even with strange sounds and unfamiliar surroundings, I slept all night without any trouble. One thing I can say about feeling this way, about sadness or depression or just being lost, a person certainly does get their rest.

My days at Holly Pines began in an uneventful manner and for the most part, continued that way. Every morning I was awakened by a nurse or attendant, ushered to the women's changing room, and allowed a nice hot shower. After getting dressed I was taken to the cafeteria for breakfast, where I encountered the other patients. I usually had oatmeal and a piece of bread and I watched as the others watched me. For the first few days, no one spoke to me and I was fine with that. In the beginning, after talking to various nurses and hospital personnel, I was tired of addressing myself to others, tired of explaining myself and numbering my feelings. I was just glad to be in a place where it looked like everyone else was worse off or at least as troubled as me. It felt like the group sessions I had attended at the university and I was glad to back among those who understood best what I could never seem to say.

Truthfully, I was comfortable at Holly Pines. I even liked my little room. Once I was settled, accepting of where I was and what I needed, once I got used to the locks and the lights, the bars on the window, and the stark emptiness inside, I made the living space into my retreat cell, my monk's chamber. When I was alone in my room I heard very little. It was mostly quiet there. I didn't feel cramped or sorry for my commitment. I was surprisingly satisfied. And before long, I found my patient's room in the psychiatric hospital to be a place of comfort and rest.

The walls were green, bright like new grass. There was a sink and a single bed, a closet, a desk and one hard-backed chair, a window with iron bars, and a door with a tiny rectangle of glass that distorted the faces of attendants and doctors who stood and watched as I slept or sat at my desk and took notes.

In my mind, to stay busy, I painted the green walls of my room. Every day a new color, a different theme. And sometimes I would make sketches in my diary of the choices I had made or the colors that I thought were especially pleasant because I considered the possibility that I might one day want to duplicate them for a friend or family member who might ask me for some decorating tips.

It didn't take long before I got the hang of how things worked at Holly Pines and I was content enough with my placement and mostly obeyed the rules. I met daily with the doctor assigned to me and was given a description of the regimen of medications I would be prescribed. "The quota," some of the other patients called it. Everybody arriving at Holly Pines is given a quota and some of us had the same one. I know this because we compared the size and colors of our pills. None of us seemed to know what they were, just whether they were tablets or capsules and who among us had the most colors in our small paper cups.

I ranked fairly low on that poll. I had only three pills. One was white, which didn't count. One was light pink and the other was blue. Mostly everyone had blue, so it was the schizophrenic with blood pressure problems and indigestion who won the rainbow award from the other patients. Apparently that was a high honor. I was never exactly sure because I tended to stay mostly with the substance abuse folks and kept a certain distance from the profoundly mentally ill ones. I don't mind a little crazy, but sometimes the way some of them could throw a tantrum just set me on edge.

I was assigned a group to meet with, others close to my age and diagnosis, depression and anxiety disorder, I believe. I met with a social worker and had a different nurse during the day and at night. There were always a handful of attendants floating around to assist. I was used to working on a staff, used to rules and a system, used to a calendar and schedule, so I had no problems with what was being asked of me. I thought I would do well as an inpatient.

After only a couple of days, however, I was labeled non-compliant because I would not eat the snack in the morning since I never like to ruin my lunch and would not play volleyball in the afternoon because the ball was too hard and left bruises on my wrists. It was because of this label on my chart, written in bold red letters, that I was moved from my first locked room and put in another, one that looked exactly like the first, a green one, but one that was farther down the hall, away from the other patients, away from the large gathering rooms, the second to the last one, on the end of the adult corridor.

As a noncompliant patient, I was kept away from the other adults during meals and free time. I was not permitted to socialize or have recreation privileges. I could no longer compete in the colored pills contest. I no longer learned of who was suddenly interested in whom. I attended group sessions, art class, grief group, and had my individual sessions, but I was not allowed to participate in the card games or the outdoor activities. I was not permitted to go on field trips and I spent most of my time alone in my room or alone in the small library.

In the library, I found myself working, of course, alphabetizing the books by the authors' last names, sorting through them to organize them by subject matter, straightening up the jackets, unfolding the dog-ears. My doctor didn't want me functioning in the same role I had on the outside, but I think the director of activities at the hospital, the staff person in charge of the library, seemed pleased to have my help. I noticed that she left the door unlocked even when the patients weren't supposed to be out of their rooms and she even asked me if I had ever set up a database on the computer.

I didn't mind the work. I found it comforting to feel useful and I liked the thought that I was keeping my ordering skills sharp. So, I lied to the doctor and told him I spent most of my time resting or writing down my dreams and not in the library organizing the books. Although I liked being by myself in a familiar setting, alone with the books, I did at times wish I had eaten my snack and played volleyball. The truth was I missed hearing the troubles of those who were hospitalized with me, having the spontaneous and unsupervised conversations that psychiatric patients have when no one on staff is watching.

For instance, during my second day at Holly Pines, I talked to a girl about twenty years old who kept pulling out clumps of her hair. We were in the group room waiting for the others. She was the first patient to speak to me.

"You a virgin?" she asked.

"What?" I replied, thinking that was a little too personal even for a crazy person to ask.

"A virgin," she repeated. "This your first time?"

"Oh," I responded, finally understanding what she meant and wondering if her hair would grow back after being yanked out in handfuls like that. I nodded.

"I could tell," she noted.

"How's that?" I asked.

"You just look like a rookie," she replied.

I nodded again. "How many times have you been here?"

"This makes my fourth time at Holly Pines." She thought about her answer. "Before that I was in a place just for young people."

"You like it here?" I asked, figuring if she kept coming back she must.

"Food's good," she responded. "And I like art class," she added.

"Why don't you just take an art class?" I asked.

And she pulled out another clump of hair and studied it. "The brushes are nice here," she responded.

And it actually made sense to me. I think most of the patients at Holly Pines are brighter than normal folks, maybe just a bit off-centered or maybe only misunderstood.

I learned later from the balding girl that one of the women being treated for bipolar disorder was stealing drugs from the other bipolar patient while no one was watching. And from one brief conversation in the television room, I discovered that the young woman who had been committed by her mother for severe behavior problems had been sexually abused by her stepfather for more than a year, but that she had never told her mother. It's just the way screwed-up people talk to one another, and I like it. And once I was not allowed to socialize, to hear the stories of the other patients, I was a little disappointed.

It didn't take long, however, to discover that if I lay very still and listened very carefully, I could hear the stories through the green walls dividing us, room by room, sorrow by sorrow. Most crazy people will eventually talk. We have to. It's the only way we keep from dying. While I listened, I knew that if I paid strict attention to the sounds, the cries and the moans, I was still able to make out the ceaseless chatter and torrid secrets of patients nearby with problems far more severe than mine.

Despite my noncompliant status, I think the doctors liked me. I answered all their questions. I was willing to discuss anything they asked. I can be quite loquacious, given the right circumstances, but generally speaking, I'm not so talkative. I keep most of my thoughts and ideas to myself. I chew on things, my mother used to say, probably still remembering me at the age of four. She says that I keep it all inside. And yet, at Holly Pines I felt a certain freedom to dig a bit deeper. I listened to what the doctors or nurses or social worker asked and I just answered it. I told them what I knew.

One doctor even commented that he was surprised that I would choose to work in a library when it appeared to him that I liked to chat so much. He found it "peculiar," he noted, that a person with such a skill for socializing would choose to build a career wrapped in silence. Obviously, it had been a long time since he had been in a library if he thought that they were places of quiet. I quit "shh-shushing" people a long time ago. It just got to be tedious and nonproductive. People are going to talk. I don't think there's anywhere that people stay quiet or talk in a whisper anymore except maybe around a dead person or when money is about to be given away. People tend to shut up at the first sign of death or if the lottery numbers are being read, but that's about it, I think.

I thought the doctor's insight about me was interesting even if it wasn't true. I'm not usually that talkative. I was just being chatty because I was in the hospital and being asked a lot of questions by a lot of different people and I am by nature a helpful person. There was also a certain freedom at Holly Pines to say things I had never said before. There is something very liberating about being in a room, in a building with lots of crazy people. Anything, it seems, goes.

I did know that this way of being with others I was exhibiting during my hospitalization, however, was not natural for me. I prefer a more quiet way of life and even if a library isn't as quiet as it used to be, it's still better than a loud office or working in a cubicle where hundreds of people talk on the phone all around you. I like a quiet workplace, an environment without a lot of clutter whether in conversation or on tables and desks. I like working alone and, of course, the other reasons I enjoy being a librarian is that I have always known a lot more about books than people, and most of all, because I love keeping things in order.

I love the system of numbers and titles, stacks of books all related by subject matter or fiction genre. I love knowing that if I learn the files, understand the rational method of where to put books on a shelf, that I can find any piece of literature in any library in any town in America. There's power in that kind of knowledge and I appreciate the magnitude of what I know. I love the Dewey decimal system with its classification rules and the simple ways to categorize. I love knowing that I am operating in the most widely used library classification system and that I can go anywhere and be an expert on how to find things. There is great comfort in that especially when I feel so lost from myself.

Even before I became a librarian, I felt at home in the quiet rooms surrounded by the bound pages of history and science, by the written biographies of explorers and adventurers. I have always loved the smell of leather bindings, the feel of paper between a finger and thumb, the crinkle of the page as it turns, the easy way life falls open from a book. As a child if I was missing, my mother always knew where to find me. I was always in the library. Later, as an adult, once I unlocked the secrets in the library and gained the knowledge that I can find any answer somebody needs, I felt great pride in my work. After all, I have a real gift for reference work and I'm confident that everybody I work with would agree with that statement.

"Go ask Andy," the other librarians would say to the researching student. "She'll know." And they were right. I usually did.

Sometimes at the university library, where I have been employed for almost a decade, students would wait for hours until I came to work just because they knew that if they had a question about anything, anything at all, I'd likely know the answer and if I didn't, I'd search all day until I could give them the right information. And once the files were computerized, the connections to every library in the world created, I was able to find stuff so fast I surprised even myself.

I also appreciate the tendency in myself that I have always given the students a little something extra too. Another name. A different direction to go. An idea about some related connection. It was like a feeling of great accomplishment to hand them my research. It made me feel important, useful, smart. So, even though library work can seem lonesome or prosaic to those who have no appreciation for the place or its tenants, I'm fully confident that my job at the library was a good match for me, a good place to settle in and work until I aged out of research.

That summer, however, that dry brown summer, when the sun was hot and unyielding, when the days wore on like grief, that summer when I felt myself falling into a hole that was long and dark and narrow, I could hardly think of my own name, Andreas Jay Hackett, much less how to find the name of the person who invented magnetic imaging or where the trunks of trees are most dense.

That summer I had become a tangle of disconnected wires, a current frayed and unmanageable, a host of uncontrollable impulses. I was surrounded by a dark, heavy cloud that grew and grew and grew until I was finally sucked up in its puffy lip of rain. And once I got to the hospital, once I sat alone in my tiny cell, once I confessed to the doctor in the emergency room that I no longer felt competent trying to take care of myself, it was clear in my mind that I needed to talk about more than just what can be found in books. I needed help and I was hopeful that I would find it at Holly Pines.

The third day I was hospitalized, a day after being labeled noncompliant and having my privileges restricted, I learned that Charlie, my boss, tried to visit me. An attendant told me. She came to my room and asked me if I knew that a tall, clumsy man running his fingers through his hair had come to see me. Although I was quite surprised Charlie had come, I knew immediately who she meant and wondered whether he was still in the waiting room. I got up to go see, but she informed me that he had been turned away by the receptionist because his name wasn't on my list.

I told her that I did not know about the visitor list. I had not realized that when you check into a psychiatric hospital you are allowed to write down the names of the people you want to see. I did not remember, I explained to her, being asked or having given such a list to Louise or Farrell. She simply shrugged. She was younger than me, fidgeted a lot when she talked to the patients. I think she felt nervous around us, but I didn't really care.

"You want him on the list?" she asked, shifting her weight from side to side as she stood in front of me. She took a strand of hair and began twirling it.

I shook my head and wanted to ask her if she had talked to one of the doctors about her tics.

"What about your mom? She's called every day."

I waited for a minute to consider the question. I shook my head again.

The attendant studied me. She knew it wasn't her job to

ask me personal questions, but she seemed curious and since her fidgeting was getting more pronounced and annoying, I explained.

"She doesn't need the bother. It's my way of giving her permission not to have to come. It's for the best."

The attendant nodded, scratched her elbow, and bit on the inside of her lips.

"We can still talk by telephone, right?" I asked.

She nodded again, a couple of times.

"Good." I smiled. Speaking on the phone was enough of a connection for me and my mother while I was trying to get better.

Later I figured it out, what had happened in my intake interview, why it was that I didn't know about the visitor list. I was asked the question about my preferred visitors right after I was given the quiz of saying the order of the presidents backward. Louise had asked the question and I had not paid attention to it. I was still trying to remember whether Fillmore came before or after Pierce and I was re-membering where I would find this information in the ref-erence books back at work. Some of the biographies of presidents are listed in one area and the books dealing with the role of the president in U.S. history are in another.

Louise, rolling her eyes and looking at the clock on the wall behind me, kept saying, "Really, that's enough. You know more than most anyway." But I wanted to name them all.

So that when she did apparently move on in the interview and ask me who I would like on my list I shouted, "Taylor, Polk, Tyler," in a fit of satisfaction, and she just thought I was saying some family member who had three names. From there she went on to known allergies and the date of my last period.

I didn't even know that I was allowed to have company. But I wouldn't have put Charlie's name on my list anyway since I might have expected a card or flowers, a book about gardening or a box of candy, but never would I have thought he would have come all the way out to Vanceboro to a loony bin to see me. I would never have expected him to leave the library and drive that far.

At that time, he still called me Ms. Hackett and blushed when he saw me walk past his office to go to the bathroom because he knew that I knew that he knew where I was going, so a visit from him to Holly Pines Psychiatric Hospital would have been a total surprise and a very awkward meeting. I was comfortable talking to doctors and other patients. I found the conversations to be quite entertaining my first few days at the hospital, but I would have immediately clammed up if Charlie had shown up in the recreation room. I think it might have set me back, although the truth is that I hadn't gotten very far in three days. The truth is, as much as I was hopeful about what was going on at Holly Pines, there was still nothing, no conversation or medication, getting to the truth of why I was even there or providing me with any means of getting back to myself.

After my noncompliant status was noted, I was moved down to the end of the north hall. Once there, I lived in room sixteen and was a patient at Holly Pines for twenty-eight days, the maximum stay covered by my medical insurance policy. During my hospitalization, I tried to stay busy most of the time. Along with organizing the hospital library, which mostly had romance novels and a few self-help books, I filled up eighty-three pages in my diary, sketches and lists mostly, had six sessions with my doctor and a few medical students, eight meetings with the social worker, daily contact with a nurse and attendant, visited ten various support group meetings for depressed people, and made a clay pot in art class.

Like the others, I was also offered religious services at Holly Pines. A chaplain made regular visits to patients who requested them and met daily with groups. There were also weekly chapel services. I declined the visits and I did not go to the spirituality support groups. And it turns out, I only went to one chapel service. Like all the other patients, I was invited each time they met, by a nurse, an Evangelical Christian who saw her work as ministry. She invited everybody and I think was reprimanded more than once by her supervisor for her fervor. It didn't seem to deter her, however, because every time she knew the chaplain had arrived, she made sure that we all knew when worship was starting. A few patients, the older ones, showed real interest and asked to be escorted to the makeshift church. I, however, didn't usually want to go.

I have never been one for church even when I went with my cousins during the summers of my childhood. And the chapel services at the hospital were always scheduled on Wednesdays, during the late morning, and I found that I enjoyed being in the courtyard, outside, when I knew most of the patients were not going to be around. It was quiet and peaceful and I preferred it to the chatter of loose prayers and fiery testimonies that you could hear as you walked by the chapel.

The one service I did attend, though, was on a Sunday night. I had been at Holly Pines more than three weeks by then and I didn't have anything else to do. They had missed the usual midday meeting because of some staff emergency and rescheduled it for the weekend. Since it was raining and the usual day of Christian worship, and since I had been called out by some of the other residents during a group session earlier that week as being unsociable, I decided to join those who were attending.

Looking back, it turned out to be the most exciting event of my time at Holly Pines. It had all of the markings of a true psychiatric hospital adventure and, well, it led up to the other events that ended up changing my life.

The service began with Ledford Gibson, who kept calling himself Jesus, beating himself on the chest and screaming, "My time has come! My time has come!" That was just before we even had a call to worship or an opening prayer. Then a young kid named Rocky started slapping himself, leaving large handprints across his cheeks, and had to be removed from the room.

Finally, when they got us all settled, Mrs. Naples, the oldest alcoholic in the place, a small slip of a woman, got carried away as we sang the first hymn and tried to run through the plate-glass window next to the piano. With that, the chaplain, an overwrought girl they sent over from the local seminary, came unglued. She lost it completely and I have to say by that point in the evening, I was truly entertained.

In the beginning of the service, the young seminarian, to her credit, seemed unbothered with Ledford's outburst and even managed the self-slapping Rocky. I was impressed with her control. She had us bow our heads and close our eyes while she called the attendant to escort the self-destructive teenager from the group. She even led a prayer while she helped remove the boy and she never dropped a word from what had been studied and memorized. But when Mrs. Naples, cut and bleeding, was still singing the words to "The Old Rugged Cross" while she ran from end to end of the room, well that scared the poor girl silly. She panicked and called off the service.

I was more than just a little disappointed. I was curious as to what would happen next. Besides, the library was locked because one of the bulimics started eating pages in the books and had to be sent to the local emergency clinic when she started to choke, and since it was raining, prohibiting us from going outside, there was nothing else to do. And even though the chaplain and the other patients seemed terribly upset about Mrs. Naples's behavior and her wounds, it didn't really bother me. After all, it was the Holiness Church where I went every summer as a child with Grandma, Aunt LuEller, PeeDee, and the others.

It was there in those girlish seasons that I had seen a snake handler bitten by a rattler and people speaking in tongues, most of them falling out after having been slain in the spirit. I had heard gospel choirs that could make the hair stand up on the back of your neck and seen baptisms that looked more like drownings. I had heard preachers preaching all about Hell and I had even witnessed an exorcism.

In my time at the Greater Union Holiness Church, I saw a bunch of people get sanctified in lots of unusual ways, so Mrs. Naples running and flopping around like a fish on the bottom of a boat didn't frighten me; I was accustomed to all that. That did not bother me at all. I was even hopeful that there would be a little more spirit before we were sent back to our rooms. I was approached by the Evangelical nurse, worried that I may have been traumatized by what had happened, but I told her I was fine. And I was. Nothing upset me at all about church until later. I didn't get anxious until I saw him.

It wasn't until Lathin Hawkins, the suicidal inmate from the state prison who came to chapel in handcuffs, bit his lip and smiled while the blood rolled down his chin, his eyes all wide and glassy, that I felt my heart race and tiny beads of sweat form along the top of my lip. Seeing the way he looked, the way he kept biting himself, now that shook me up. That was what ultimately called off church for me.

Later, walking back to my room, still struck by what I had felt from the man in the wheelchair, I learned that it was not usual for a prisoner to be at Holly Pines. I would have guessed that, but not having been in a psychiatric facility before I wasn't sure about patient protocol. As I walked around the corner, however, I saw some of the staff whispering to each other, so I stopped near the desk to get the real scoop, to hear what was being said.

I heard Louise tell Cathy, the nurse in training, that the

prison couldn't keep the inmate in the infirmary and that Dorothea Dix down in Raleigh didn't have a bed for him until after the weekend. Then she added something like, "You know how that son of a bitch will do anything for money," and she rolled her eyes and laughed. I figured she was talking about the Holly Pines executive director. He struck me as just that kind of man.

I met Mr. Willis the day after I arrived at the hospital and when it was confirmed that my insurance company approved of my stay. He had congratulated me for addressing my needs and making my mental health a priority. Even in the early fog of my "quota" it was easy to see that he was a man who liked to make money. Putting two and two together, I'm sure that the other facilities denied the inmate inpatient status. However, once it was decided tax money from the prison system would be siphoned to the private hospital, Mr. Hawkins was welcomed to Holly Pines and the warden was informed that he could stay on the north-side hall in room eighteen at the end by himself and that none of us would even know that he was there. The census was down anyway, the lowest I had seen it since I arrived, and it seemed that everybody on staff was told that it would only be for a couple of days, just weekend care. He had already been there an entire day and night without incident.

Since the inmate's records were sealed for most of the employees on duty at Holly Pines, the weekend attendant didn't realize that Lathin wasn't supposed to leave his room when he wheeled him into the multipurpose room for the chapel service. And it wasn't until the chaplain called the code red and all the nurses came running into the middle of the room that it was noticed that Mr. Lathin Hawkins, number 7765982, was out of his room and in a public space where he was not supposed to be. There seemed to be as much panic from the staff about that as there was about Mrs. Naples.

I got a good look at him before they wheeled him out. A lonesome-looking man, eyes fixed on something from too long ago, he filled up the space around him. His skin was as dark as chocolate and his hair was tight curls of black and white, a full slope of knots.

He was tall, skinny. I could tell this even with him sitting down because his knees rested high, almost above his chest, his legs trying to fit into that amount of room the wheelchair provided. His arms were bandaged and his shoulders were draped over the situation of his heart. He had on black military boots, spit-shined leather, an odd finish to the otherwise disheveled look that he wore.

He saw me staring at him when Roy unlocked his wheels and pushed him out of the group. I felt him watch me see me as if he knew me. He opened his mouth like he was going to speak, an O formed, but was not said. And then he just stuck out his tongue and licked the pool of blood that ran from the corner of his bottom lip. And then he spun his head around and hissed at the skinny chaplain who was screaming about how crazy we all were. She was so disturbed by Mrs. Naples's surge through the back window, she didn't even notice, but I did.

The attendant jerked the chair and Lathin was thrown forward, falling on his too-tall knees, like a dog on all fours.

Roy pulled him back into the chair by the collar of his denim shirt and wheeled him out the door, his fingers waving as he went into the hall. I thought he was signaling to me.

It wasn't until later that night when the lights went out and all of the doors were locked and checked, that Lathin Hawkins and I broke the rules and spoke to each other through the sobs of a teenager at the other end of the hall and the vent next to the bottom of the bed.

It wasn't until the moths circled the streetlamp, flitting about like the souls of children, and the black night stood outside my window, close and pinched, that I learned about his crime and the way his daughter used to catch drops of rain in her tiny cupped hands and whisper the names of flowers in her sleep. It wasn't until darkness drank in the light, covering us all like a thick, heavy veil that I felt as if for the first time in a long time I could actually find myself again.

And it wasn't until then, a late hour in the day and a late hour in my Holly Pines stay, that I started feeling better, started to sense the power of hope. It wasn't until then that I finally began to see the slightest edge of light breaking around the fist of darkness that was my heart.

It wasn't until then, beginning almost at midnight on a Sunday night, just a few hours before I was going to be discharged, that a conversation with a prison inmate down at the end of the hall broke open the loose and lost memories in my life and things finally began to fall back in order.

THREE

362.28

$\mathcal{S}$UICIDE

"Hey," Lathin spoke and then everything went quiet.

"Can you hear me over there?"

I followed the whisper to the corner of my room, but didn't yet know how to respond. I figured it was him. I didn't move from where I was sitting.

I had heard all of the conversation at the nurses' station between Louise and that new girl. Once I left the chapel service, I stopped going in the direction of my room and walked over to the sofa in the main room near the station and sat down. I was supposed to be watching television, but I knew they would be discussing what had just happened. So, I stayed.

In my time at Holly Pines I discovered discretion is rarely practiced around crazy people. Most of the staff members just assume we're all too screwed up to understand what they're talking about. I've learned a lot just from sitting near the nurses' station and the employee lounge.

The television program was some sitcom about two men raising a son, but I wasn't following what was so funny about a house without women because I was really paying attention to Louise and Cathy talk about whether or not they were going to inform the director that the inmate had been taken from his room. Louise was leaning in the direction of "less information is best" on the nightly report, but Cathy seemed to want to follow the rules.

"Maybe that would keep him from doing this again," Cathy said. She was flushed and probably not so happy about having to care for a prisoner. She was referring to the executive director.

"Willis will bring in the Devil if his premiums are paid." Louise struck me as saucy the first time I met her. It was clear that she was well informed of the lay of the land at Holly Pines. I waited for more dialogue, but the two women seemed to have said all they were going to say about the prison inmate matter.

Once the prisoner had been returned, Roy, the attendant, came over to the station. Cathy stood nearby while he was reprimanded by Louise for not obeying the notice on the inmate's chart. It was clearly written in large red letters, she pointed out, the other nurse seeming a bit embarrassed for him: DO NOT ALLOW PATIENT TO LEAVE ROOM.

Roy said he couldn't find the chart when he went down to pick up the man's food tray, and he said, loud enough for

everyone in the television room and in the halls close by to
hear him, "I'm not a damn police officer. I don't get paid
enough for this shit."

I turned to watch Louise slam the chart and order Roy to
go clean up the mess still in the chapel. Cathy moved over
near the file cabinets and out of the way. I pretended not to
know anything, even gave a chuckle on cue with the audience watching the sitcom. I was trying to blend in, but I
guess it didn't work.

After my chuckle, Louise noticed me and said I should be
in my room. Without responding, I left to go to bed. Once
inside, I began listening for the sounds from the room next
door. I knew from having seen Roy take the man through
the door next to mine that he was right beside me. I was curious about him, interested in what he was doing at Holly
Pines, why he had bandages on his arms, and if he was going to stay a long time there.

However, before answering him, since he had asked me a
question, I had to consider the consequences of engaging in
a conversation with a man from prison. After all, I thought,
maybe he was a serial killer and would find out where I lived,
escape someday, and wait for me. There were definite risks
involved if I participated in a dialogue with the new patient.
I had to think things through before just jumping in and
starting to talk to the man. And then, maybe he wouldn't say
anything else. Maybe, I thought, he had decided not to try
and talk to me.

I walked over and stared at the vent beside the bed, this

tunnel to a man calling out to me, this passageway to another life.

"Y'all finish church?"

Silence.

I would have to decide whether to talk to him or not. I walked to the end of the bed near the vent, farther along the wall, and sat down. I was facing the length of the room. I could hear him humming, so lightly that I could not recognize the tune.

"Won't really a service anyway," he responded to himself. "She didn't seem much like a preacher."

There was a pause. I guess he was still waiting for me to say something.

"We got a good preacher at Central," he kept on, talking about the prison, I guess.

"I think the church he was at let him go because he kept sleeping with all the choir members, but he sure can preach."

I heard him slide down. There was a slight thud that made me think he had landed.

"Make them big ole men cry like babies."

I was sure his back was up against the wall just like mine, and I thought about his weight resting next to me. I wondered if he was relaxed in room eighteen, wondered if he was glad to be away from prison walls, wondered how crazy he was.

"First time I heard him, he preached about the woman who got caught shacking. You know that Jesus story?"

I didn't say anything. I had not yet made up my mind about being friendly, but I did know the story. I learned the Bible really well when I went to church. Besides, I kind of have a photographic memory when it comes to stories and things in books.

"The church folk dragging her to the center of the town for her to be pistol-whipped? You remember?"

He seemed to be listening for a minute, but then continued.

"Oh, now that man preached that story like he was there. He described it down to her torn linen dress and hair all ragged and pulled loose. The church people all high and puffed up with themselves, folks standing around watching with the full light of the sun on their deed. Yeah, he told it like he knew it, like he felt it deep inside himself."

Then he stopped.

"You ever hear preaching like that?"

I nodded, thinking about a Baptist preacher from Rose Hill, but I didn't say it out loud. We only went to his church a couple of times, but I remembered him like I had been a member of his church. He was just that good. He wasn't scary, though, didn't tell everybody we were all going to hell. He was just good at making you want to know what happened next. I think Mama went to talk to him a couple of times, but he never came visiting like Holiness preachers. I'm not sure what Mama told him, but whatever it was it must have frightened him away. We moved not long after visiting his church, but I will never forget how he preached.

"He said she wasn't even scared anymore because she

had given up her soul when she slept with the man she knew would betray her, that her heart was already dried-up like an old bone and her eyes were cold and empty, that she didn't fight or scream, she just let them pull her along."

He made that humming noise again.

" 'Nobody's mother and nobody's child,' he said, 'she was a woman of the dust.' Mmm-mmm," Lathin added.

"Then the preacher said, as they were just about to break her neck with the stones, they saw Jesus, the wandering rabbi who claimed to know everything and who confounded everybody."

Lathin paused.

"And that's when the preaching got real good."

He started to whisper.

"He moved out in front of his pulpit and got right down with us men, eye to eye, face-to-face. And he said, 'And they told of her to Jesus. And Jesus knew the woman's plight, but he was not turned away.' "

Lathin had a drawl now, like the black preachers I have heard in revival.

He repeated himself, softer this time, like the chorus being sung by a choir. "And Jesus knew the woman's plight, but he was not turned away."

I tried to push the bed away from the vent and toward the door, giving me more room, but discovered that the hospital staff had bolted the frame to the floor.

In all my days in that room and in the first one before I was punished and sent down here, I had not noticed this before and suddenly I quit listening to Lathin to think about why my bed wouldn't move. I guess I hadn't ever been down on the floor before and I hadn't tried to push the furniture. After considering the purpose for a bolted bed, I decided it was for security reasons, though I couldn't see what a crazy person could do with a bed.

"And then he said, 'And Jesus got down on his knees, his eyes taking in all that was around him, the woman and her ripped dress, her busted soul, the crowd and their pleasure in her killing, and the air went quiet as they all held their breath at what he was going to do to the woman who was to be stoned.'"

He was still talking and I wondered if I had missed anything. I quit thinking about the bed.

"And then the preacher got down on his knees too and looked at us all, man after man, then again to the woman he said lay at Jesus' feet. And then that preacher man bent down and began to stroke her hair and pull the straps of her dress across her shoulders, giving her back some of her dignity, and I swear we saw her there. It was like she was down at his feet."

He hesitated for a minute, remembering the sermon, I figured.

"Tears filled his eyes, and he lifted up his face to us and shouted hard and low, 'Let the one who has not wronged another throw out the first rock.'"

It was silent for a few moments.

"And then he said, 'And Jesus cradled the woman and her broken heart and her dried-up soul and waited to be stoned with her.'"

I heard the smile in his voice.

"Ah, it was something," he said. "A sermon, like I ain't never heard."

Then he made a noise like a snort, a sigh. "Now you see, that's preaching."

There was another few minutes when he didn't speak and I wondered if the men in prison gave their hearts to Jesus because of such a sermon as this. I wondered whether Lathin changed his ways after hearing it. I wondered if the preacher believed it all himself and thought he would go to Heaven for bringing salvation to rough and broken criminals.

"You think it was because she's a woman?" I asked.

"What?" he responded, sounding surprised that I had finally answered him.

He cleared his throat. "You mean about Jesus?"

"No, that the chaplain wasn't able to preach. Was it because she's a woman?"

"Oh, no, that ain't it. I heard some women preach that would make the Devil die on a cross."

I pulled a pillow off my bed and pushed it behind me and leaned my head against the wall.

"She just doesn't have the Holy Ghost is all. Lots of preachers preach, but they ain't got no Ghost."

"How do you get the Ghost?" I asked, thinking that for a prison inmate, he sure knew a lot about preaching.

"God decides," he said confidently.

"And you got to want it, can't be afraid of it," he added.

I considered his notion. "Only preachers get it?" I asked.

"Ah, hell no. Anybody can get it. Preachers just the ones who've figured out how to make a dollar with it."

I smiled and nodded. Maybe he was crazy, but he was making a whole lot of sense to me.

"I'm talking real low right now so as not to call attention to ourselves, but I can make my voice sound like a preacher, like big cracks of thunder. That's how I've managed to stay alive all this time."

He waited before going on.

" 'Course that's also how I sometimes get myself into trouble. I learned it from my father, a little skinny man who beat women and ended up with a kitchen knife stuck in his neck by my uncle."

I cringed at that.

"My daddy died from that cut and Uncle Jeter spent three years at a work camp, busting rock and pulling tobacco."

I heard him try to move his bed. I thought to tell him about the bolts, but I knew that he would figure it out the same way I did. Finally, I heard him give up.

"All the men I know is dead or chained," Lathin said, his voice like a distant storm. "Dead or chained," he whispered again to himself as if he had said this a hundred times.

"Your daddy dead?" he asked.

"I don't know," I said, talking into the green corner of my room, not the least bit offended that he asked, surprised that nobody had asked me that before. In the entire time that I had been at Holly Pines nobody seemed to want to know about my father.

"I pretend he died when I was a baby."

"You make up that somebody killed him?"

I shook my head at first and then I remembered that he couldn't see me. "No. I believe he was just sick, passed sometime when I wasn't there to see him."

Lathin didn't respond and I wondered what he was looking at in his room, if the paint was fresh and smeared into the door frame like it was in mine, whether he was handcuffed to his bed, and if his lip was still bleeding.

"Your mama raise you by herself?"

A door slammed at the end of the hall and the teenager who had slapped himself during chapel started cursing. Another voice challenged. There was a loud noise like something being thrown against the wall.

I waited to answer until it was quiet. Three voices escalated, then there was a shuffle and finally silence. The teenager was moved to another room. It had happened before. It was as if they could never decide where he was supposed to sleep.

"Yeah, mostly," I recalled and then I thought about the summers at Grandma's with Aunt LuEller and all her children, but I didn't mention them. "We moved quite a bit."

"Nothing wrong with moving," Lathin replied. "I've lived in twelve states and thirty-nine cities. All of them got they own story, they own sunrise, they own women."

"What's your favorite?" I asked.

"What? Story or sunrise? I know you ain't asking me about the women?"

I laughed, but only slightly. It wasn't that funny.

"City," I said. "What's your favorite city?"

He waited a minute, thinking, I supposed.

"I guess, if I had to name it, my favorite would have to be Dubois, Wyoming." Then he made a humming noise. "You ever been to Wyoming?"

"No," I said, for it was true, I had never been there. I had been in lots of place, but none of them any great distance from Mama's hometown. She liked the thought of being adventurous and getting away from her parents, but truthfully, she never had the courage to go very far.

"Oh, the sky is big out there, like it's another layer of atmosphere or something. Another shade of blue. Another ceiling to the Earth or floor of Heaven dipping just low enough for us to peek into the playgrounds of angels."

He was quiet for a minute, and I imagined him smiling to himself, his big split lip stretching wide over his teeth.

"Weren't many black people," he said. "But it didn't matter. There was so much time and land between everybody, you just felt glad to see another human being when one came across your path. White, black, Crow, or Shoshone, they all felt like kin."

He stopped when we heard the door open and close at the other end of the hall.

I got up quickly, carrying the pillow, and lay on the bed, my face toward the wall. I was used to the nightly visits. I knew they came in about four times a night and checked on the patients.

There were steps and soon I felt the stare of someone

peeking at me through the glass in the door. And then the feeling was gone.

Steps went to Lathin's room, stopped, and then I heard them again down the hall. The door closed. I counted a few breaths and then I returned to the corner, taking my pillow with me.

He picked up right where he had left off.

"I ranched cattle for a cowboy named Houston. It was just me, two hundred longhorns, that great big sky, and the voices of dead people that trailed down the Wind River Mountain Range. I had a little shanty out in the middle of nowhere, and sometimes it would get so lonesome I thought I could decipher what the ghosts were saying."

I wondered how that sounded, but I didn't ask.

"Once in a while a body'd ride through, but mostly it was just me and them cows. 'Course, things probably changed by now. Last time I was out there was '76."

I heard two loud thumps and figured he was taking off his shoes or moving closer to the vent.

"Were you born yet?"

"You mean in '76?" I asked.

"Yeah. How old are you?"

"Maybe you could guess." I wanted to see what he knew.

"I figure you were born in the seventies. You seem about like you're cresting on your early years. Probably in the late winter you came out, made a hard labor for your mama."

"You think that's why I'm crazy?"

"I don't know, you crazy?"

I thought that it was nice that he asked, that he didn't just assume that about me because of where we met. I wasn't like that. I just assumed everybody at Holly Pines was not normal, off center, crazy.

Even though he couldn't see me, I shrugged. And then I thought about how my coming into the world might shape how I saw things, how I measured things, and I thought about Mama saying I was a slow baby. Kept starting out then changing my mind. I was two weeks late and even then had to be pulled out with force, with forceps wrapped around the crown of my head.

Mama said my skull was curved until I was three years old because of the way the doctor had to yank me out. I guess I was just comfortable where I was. I still don't know if that was what started my personality.

"Yeah, I was born around then," I said, surprised that he knew, surprised that he had seen enough of me at the chapel service to figure that out. I waited, wondering if I wanted to say anything else about that, wondering if there was some clue in the time of my birth. I shook my head.

"But spring had already come. And I don't figure I was hard or anything. I think I was a happy enough child."

Images of myself floated across my mind. School pictures from kindergarten through junior high. The different haircuts, inspired by the teenagers, the frilly dresses when I was a little girl and then boys' shirts and blue jeans, which was all that I would wear when I was a young teenager. The dim light that was my eyes.

"Yeah, I suppose most children find a way to be happy even in the worst situations."

"You try to commit suicide?" I had heard enough from the conversation at the nurses' station to surmise that about him.

"Yeah."

There was a sigh in the silence, distant but distinguishable.

"I figured I was ready to go."

"You try to hang yourself?"

That's how I heard most prisoners killed themselves, tied their sheet around their necks and wound it around something on the ceiling, a beam or light fixture. And then, suddenly I thought maybe that was why you couldn't move the bed. Maybe somebody had tried standing on the bed to hang themselves and they pushed the bed away, leaving their body dangling at the end of a bedsheet. Of course, that didn't explain why the chair wasn't bolted.

I didn't see if Lathin was wearing a belt. Some of them did it with belts. I remembered reading this for a student who was writing a paper for the criminal justice class. I also knew that at Holly Pines we weren't allowed to have belts. I figure it was for that very reason.

"No."

I wondered if he was going to explain, but didn't expect it. He certainly didn't have any reason to tell me his methods.

"I bought a blade from a man named T-Bone. He buys and sells most of the stuff in-house. He's got about anything you need, cigarettes, cards, posters. I suppose I wasn't the first one to ask about a knife, but when he found out I didn't need it for protection or carving wood or something, he told a guard and they got to me before I was finished."

"You did it, then?" I asked and turned my head. The wall was cold against my face as I considered the memory of his blood that had spilled down his shirt.

"Mmm-mmm." He said it so low that I almost didn't hear him. "I burned my ropes pretty good."

I waited before I spoke, suddenly recalling the thick white bandages wrapped around his arms, thinking about despair pumping through veins.

"I got a knife one time," I replied, telling the thing that had never been said, not even considering why it was I was now telling it to him. Of course, I had been asked about that by the medical staff, but it was so long ago I hadn't considered it relevant to what was going on then. Maybe I should have told someone else.

"Held it so that the blade rested against my skin in that soft place on the inside of your arm." I thought how it had felt like the tip of a sharp tongue.

"I learned that you cut long ways down the vein if you want to die quick." I added this in case he didn't think I knew.

I closed my eyes and remembered.

"It was seven P.M., a Tuesday. I had just watched *Jeopardy!* and heard the Final Jeopardy clue and I knew it. I knew the answer. Who is William Jennings Bryan?"

"I don't know, who is William Jennings Bryan?" Lathin asked.

"He was the one who made the 'Cross of Gold' speech at the Democratic Party convention in 1896."

"What's a 'Cross of Gold' speech?"

" 'You shall not crucify mankind upon a cross of gold.' He was talking about the gold money in the late 1800s. He sided with the poor farmers and thought the country should build up the budget with more silver coins. He didn't win the presidency, of course."

"Nobody who sides with the poor people ever does."

I agreed.

"Anyway, none of the contestants knew it, and the guy who won the match only got twelve dollars because he had bet so much. But still, they all applauded and congratulated him like he had won thousands."

Lathin was listening.

"I stood up and turned off the TV feeling all proud of myself somehow, all satisfied. And then suddenly after that rush of knowing the right answer, lost in that false sense of assurance that people like to think will save them, I felt finished in some way, completed, like that was it."

I heard him make a noise that made me think he understood.

"I drew a little blood, but I don't know, it just seemed too messy, too wasteful, all that blood gathering and sticking to the floor. I decided I didn't want to be remembered like that, opened up and falling out of myself. So I sliced up an apple instead and rearranged the books on my shelves."

I started thinking about the books, all neat and dusted, alphabetized by the author's last name.

"I never watched *Jeopardy!*" he said like he was answering a survey. "Guess it's a good show, lots of folks eat their suppers by it."

"Yeah, it's company," I said, thinking of all the nights I curled up with my Lean Cuisine wondering how many answers Alex Trebek knows before he reads the cards.

"Mary liked TV."

"That your wife?" I asked.

"No, that's my baby. Felicia was my old lady. She left us when we moved back to Georgia."

"What kind of TV did Mary like?" I thought that she could be any age by now. She could be a little girl or she could be grown, like me.

Lathin had to be about sixty or so, just to have done all that he made it sound like he had done, living in Wyoming, getting locked up in prison. Plus, he looked old.

"Cartoons mostly, and the game shows. She liked the game shows."

"Yeah?" I asked. "The ones where smart people win or the ones where everybody has the same chance?"

"*Price Is Right,*" he replied. "Mostly, she liked *The Price Is Right.*"

"Mmm," I said in reply.

A tree stood right outside my window, and a late wind

blew its full limbs against the glass. Shadows danced like flames about the room.

"Mary liked the women on that game show, all teeth and tits. She liked the way they draped their arms around washing machines and ski boats, looking like they was greeting long-lost family members. Thinking she might one day grow up to be like them, even though there wasn't a black woman among them. She still thought it would be possible that she could drive to Hollywood and walk up to Bob Barker, and point herself right into television."

He laughed as the air conditioner hummed behind the conversation like background music. They kept it cool at Holly Pines. I think they thought crazy people sweated more than others. I had asked for an extra blanket the first night I was there.

"Crazy girl. I'd come home from getting fired from a job or losing a card game and she'd jump up from the sofa and start hugging the TV set or the recliner, talking about, 'Here, Daddy, here's you a brand-new velvet chair.' Then she sit down in it all Miss America–like and pop it back and wave her hands in the air like she was directing a choir.

" 'This is all yours,' she'd say, ' 'cause the price is right.' Then she'd smile and twirl that chair around like she was rich. And Lord, even I started to think it was all going to be all right. And we'd open a can of Vienna sausages and a pack of stale crackers and eat like we was a king and his queen."

There was a long pause and I thought maybe Lathin had

fallen off to sleep. It reminded me of the summers of my childhood when PeeDee would stop right in the middle of a ghost story and be deep asleep, snoring. "PeeDee," I'd call out, waiting to hear the story, waiting to know what happened to the dead woman who lost her head at the railroad tracks and whether or not she ever got peace. But PeeDee had talked herself to sleep. She wouldn't even remember the story the next morning when I'd ask her for the ending. She was just that way, full of imagination. I had always envied the way she could make up stories without time to think.

"'Course, that was then and this is now," he said, his words resounding in the silence. He was still awake.

"Yep," I said, because it was true.

"You talk to the doctors here?"

"I guess," I replied, remembering the stone face of the one I had seen earlier that day. He had not heard a thing I said the entire time we talked. I knew this because in the middle of answering one of his questions I had told him that I enjoyed the taste of dirt. He didn't even stop to ask me what I had just said, just kept reading whatever file he had in front of him. One of the other patients, the bipolar girl, told me to try it with him. So, I did. We had a good laugh afterward. She said that she had told him she was really an alien, up from Roswell, New Mexico. He didn't even look up when she said it.

"They help you?"

"Not really," I said back, thinking about the sad girl who really did need somebody to listen, somebody to help her.

"It's like they think they know what I'm supposed to say before I get asked anything. And so if I answer something in the way they weren't expecting, they change the question around to get what they wanted."

I paused. I wasn't sure he understood. It was kind of complicated to explain. Mama had not followed me at all when I told her the same thing during a phone conversation we had earlier that week.

"Do you know what I mean?"

Lathin snorted. And I took that for affirmation.

"Dr. Thibendeaux asked me the day before yesterday if I ever had nightmares and I said, 'How do you know the difference between a really bad dream and a nightmare?' And he said, 'Nightmares wake you up and leave you short of breath and sweaty.' So I said, 'Then do you want to know if I have bad dreams or if I wake up short of breath and sweaty?' And he said, 'Do you wake up short of breath and sweaty?' And I said, 'No, I don't, and why didn't you just ask me that in the first place?' And then he wrote something down on his paper like he knew all the time what I was going to say. He wasn't even listening to me."

"Do you have bad dreams?" Lathin followed up closely.

"Yeah," I said quietly. "But not the kind you think."

"What kind of bad dreams do I think?" he asked.

"Spiders and snakes. Drowning and falling down elevator shafts. The man-chasing-a-woman kind of dream. The ones where you can't run or can't dial 911. That kind."

"Yeah," Lathin replied, "that's pretty much the kind I think."

"Yeah, most people do," I said.

"So, what kind do you have?"

I did not respond. I closed my eyes, remembering. It was not something of which I ever spoke out loud.

I thought about the blue-black color, the smell of damp bundles of pine needles. The way the night sky will widen and thicken into distorted images and grotesque shapes. The sounds of old leaves stirred about and how darkness can grow a face.

I thought about the way I woke up, the feeling of death, the way my heart felt squeezed inside my chest. I thought about the voice calling me, the light misting of rain, the way I begged to wake up. But none of these things could I tell him. I was not ready to say.

"You dream?" I asked softly.

Lathin didn't say anything about why I didn't answer him.

"About Mary mostly or getting out of prison. I don't have a lot of bad dreams. Guess what's real is enough of that."

"Where is she now?" I asked.

"I don't know. Haven't seen her in twenty-one years."

"Is that why you dream about her? Because you don't know where she is?"

"Maybe."

He stopped and I thought perhaps we had said too much too fast.

I had a date like that when I was young, one where you spoke too much too fast. I was eighteen or nineteen and met a guy in a bookstore. He was tall, lanky, seemed uncomfortable with himself. I thought that quality of his was charming so I agreed to go out with him later that evening. He picked me up at the corner near where I lived.

Right away we started sharing secrets about what we were like as children, even the things about which we were most embarrassed, and somehow, by the time we had arrived at the restaurant, not even an hour later, we were suddenly uncomfortable with each other. It was as if there were nothing else for us to say to each other. It was like telling some stranger on an airplane all the things you wouldn't say to your closest friend and then finding out you're going to the same conference or staying at the same hotel. It's unnerving to keep going when you went too far to start with.

I told him I had a stomachache and he took me right home. We never went out again. And I think he was always disgusted with himself for telling me about the time he wet his pants at a baseball game.

"Mary was nine when I got sent to jail. Felicia was in a drunk tank somewhere so her sister took her. We kept in touch for a while. They'd bring her to see me and she'd write me little notes with pictures of the house where she was staying and the dog. Big daisy flowers and fat valentine hearts. I kept them in the Bible the Gideons gave us. Tore out the whole New Testament just so there'd be room for all of 'em in there."

It sounded like he slid over toward his bed. I heard bedding rumple and fall.

"They're real strict about how much stuff you can take with you when you're shipped out to another yard."

He yawned. I could hear the sound of his breath, drawn and expelled.

"I dream about her from then, not how she'd be now."

"Tell me," I said, as I lay down on my side by the wall and closed my eyes, feeling somewhat sleepy.

"I bought her this little lavender dress the day I won at the dog races in Charleston. That was when we moved to West Virginia because a buddy had told me about the Union Carbide plant hiring a lot of extra men. After I won, I picked her up from the babysitter's and I told her she could buy anything she wanted, thinking she'd want some tea set or china doll."

Lathin was talking slow like he was telling it to someone writing it all down. I wondered if he had ever told this before. I wondered if someone had written it down before.

He continued. "But on our way to the toy store we walked past this dress place, this real fancy store with spring dresses and hats to match. Easter dresses, they looked like, with the clothes display made up to look like a garden. And she just stopped and stared in the window like it was a museum or a church."

I took a long stretch and then opened my eyes, trying to stay awake. I patted my hands against my face. I wasn't used to staying up this late.

"I asked her if she wanted to go in there and she eyed me like I was asking her if she wanted to have her liver taken out."

He stopped, remembering, I guess.

"Her face got all knotted up and she shook her head and

started backing away from the window like she was scared, like she was really scared."

There was nothing and the silence seemed to wake me up.

"She looked down at what she was wearing, some blue-jeaned shorts and a T-shirt that I thought was fine, maybe a bit too small, 'cause she was sprouting up like a weed, but there wasn't anything wrong with it. And I said, 'What is it, baby?' And she would just look up at me and then again at her clothes and back to the window."

Lathin stopped, the silence thick with memory.

"And then I realized. She thought she couldn't go into that dress store. She thought she wasn't allowed."

I moved closer, my ear almost at the wall. I could hear him fiddling with something, paper, I thought.

"I knew me or her mama had never carried her into that kind of place; that most of her clothes were hand-me-downs from cousins or neighbors or that they came from yard sales or discount stores. But I didn't know that she thought she couldn't go into a store like that, that somehow she believed she wasn't good enough to walk into some fancy girls' place."

I imagined him standing with his little girl in front of some downtown boutique, young and angry, blaming himself somehow for his daughter's embarrassment.

"A baby shouldn't have to think things like that. Little ole baby girl like that thinking she wasn't allowed to wear lacy clothes or something new with the tag still hanging on it. Little girl like that shouldn't already know those kind of things."

It went quiet for a minute.

"Little bitty thing like that."

And the story stopped.

I dropped my head, suddenly remembering a time when I was about six years old.

I had gotten up early that morning because there was a thunderstorm. We were living in a trailer then, somewhere in the eastern part of the state, and thunderstorms always made me afraid. There was only one bedroom, so every night Mama would make the sofa into a bed for me since I always got up first and liked to watch cartoons. She slept in the back and shut her door since she didn't like to be woken up real early.

The storm was rocking the trailer and I got off the sofa and pulled out the blanket, dragging it behind me, thinking I would get in the bed with her, which was something I did fairly regularly anyway.

I opened the bedroom door and as I rubbed the sleep from my eyes, I saw that Mama wasn't by herself in the bed. I stood there just watching as she woke up and saw me, then shook this strange man until he was awake.

I stood and watched as he finally got up and put on his pants and stood up by the bed. He pulled out his wallet from his back pocket and placed a fifty-dollar bill on the dresser and patted my head as he walked out past me. I followed him with my eyes as he walked out the front door and then I turned to see Mama's face, which was the color of ashes, gray and flaked, her eyes full of something I didn't understand.

All of a sudden, she pulled her glance away from me, real hard and fast, and covered her face with the sheet. I stood at the bedroom door for a minute, not understanding what had happened, not understanding why she was crying, and then I crawled in the bed next to her and spooned myself around her as close as I could. And as the storm beat about that old trailer and the roof leaked, causing the rain to puddle in the corners, my mama cried an ocean, the tears soaking her pillow and filling up the bed. Without knowing its name or all of its consequences, that was the time I learned the meaning of shame.

"Well, we went into that store," Lathin began again, startling me from the memory.

"Her walking so close behind me that I felt her shallow breath on the backs of my legs. And I bought her that lavender dress that was hanging in the window even though she claimed she didn't want it."

I rubbed my eyes and rolled over.

"It was real pretty with little white flowers and a long purple satin ribbon that tied around the waist. I kept asking her didn't she want to try it on, since I didn't know too much about her size, but she just stood with her face hard against me, trying to disappear.

"Even the saleslady was real nice to her," he continued. "And a white woman too. Even she tried to get Mary to stand away from me so she could at least hold it up to her, but my little baby wouldn't budge."

It was a few minutes before he said something else. The words were muffled, hard to make out.

"Mary never put on that dress. It hung in her closet with the plastic wrap still on it. She never even took it off the rack."

I listened intently to hear what he said, and I thought about a little girl's dress and the tiny ways we try to make life fair.

"That was the first place I burned down when I started messing with fire."

I let the quiet, heavy words sit for a minute. I did not know what to do with his confession. It wasn't that it shocked me or caused me to fear him; after more than three weeks at Holly Pines, I had already heard a lot of stories more horrible than having to do with arson. I just thought what he said needed some space to settle. So, I waited.

"That why you're in prison?"

"One of the reasons," he replied, his voice a little stronger now. "Why are you in?"

I had to smile. I guess he knew I wasn't in prison, but I suppose from the inside out, any institution must feel like jail.

"I'm not sure," I said, at least trying to be honest. After telling what he just told, I felt as if I owed him that. And then, I told him the rest of the truth, what I did know.

"I stood very close to the edge of a deep hole for a long time, thinking I could fall in, but never really knowing how to keep it from happening." I pulled my arms behind my head and slid my feet up to make a table with my knees.

"Then, one day, it just did, happen I mean. I fell in, headfirst and long."

I turned my face toward the wall. "And that's where I've been ever since."

The wind rustled through the tree by the window again and I turned to watch the shadows on the wall.

"Your mama know you're here?"

"Yep."

"She come to see you?"

"No."

"Mmm," he said, a sympathetic gesture.

"I asked her not to." Trying to explain that it wasn't because she didn't care, trying to defend her absence. It really wasn't her fault.

"She's sort of frail and all. I think maybe it's best she not see me when I'm like this. We talk on the phone," I added, like that was worth something.

I propped one leg across the other and began to think about how my mother managed the year I was sixteen. Nervous like a bird, her eyes darting about for signs of any improvement. Her herbal remedies and foot rubs, endless cups of ginger tea, the crayons and books, and always the question, "You all right?"

It became her mantra. She said it constantly, a thousand times a day. She must have fallen asleep to these words, awakened to the words, "You all right?" "You all right?" "You all right?" Until finally after weeks of the endless question, I screamed at her, "No, I am not all right and quit asking me that!"

It was the most enthusiastic I had been in months, the most words I had strung together in days. And reflecting upon it as I did there in that cold green room, darkness a cover about me, a friendly voice so close in my ear, I suddenly realized that my complaint, my scream blasted against my mother's frenzy, the energy propelled meant to silence her weak and flimsy lifesaving techniques, was ultimately the force that had actually pushed the stone of sorrow just enough so that the smallest sliver of hope had gotten through.

Of all the things she had tried, the smothering tenderness, the long hours she lay at my bedroom door like a shepherd guarding her sheep, the thick and messy maternal warmth she wrapped around and around my bare arms, the new sharp crayons, it was the repetition of this question like a prayer on rosary beads that finally pulled me out of my grave and caused me to take in new air.

Although she had never admitted such a thing, I knew that she was wounded by my severity and broken by my cruel response, but she would not let that emotion control her. She threw herself at my feet, her heart torn in bloody ribbons, and she thanked God that it had been enough. She sacrificed even her need to be loved just to see me return to myself.

I thought about her, how she looked that evening draped across my feet and a tear fell and slid down my face. I didn't even bother to wipe it. I liked the way the water felt, a small stream in a wash of such a disappointing life.

Lathin was quiet for a very long time. I had almost considered that the conversation was over, but I got up to pull the blanket and sheets off the bed to make myself a pallet by the vent just in case we weren't through. I didn't know if he was sleepy or not, but I knew I still had things I wanted to say.

"My mama only came to see me once, about ten years ago. I think she's in a home somewhere."

I was glad he was still in the mood to talk and I wondered if it would be possible for me to move the mattress on the floor and I glanced over to the bed to study it. I was about to ask him her age.

"She was old then," he added.

I nodded and then decided moving the mattress would be too much trouble. I knew the night attendant would be back to check on me in a couple of hours. It would be a lot easier to put the linens back on the bed.

"Why do you think she didn't come see you again?" I asked.

"She hated coming to the farm. She'd got all nervous-acting, pulling at her coat collar, looking around the room like she was waiting to be jumped, guarding her purse like she thought a brother was gonna throw her down and take her check. I guess it was just too much for her."

I unfolded the sheets and put the blanket on top, and then I slid between them. I thought about Lathin's mother and my mother and wondered how their conversation might go if they ever found themselves talking together about their children. "She's a good girl," I imagined my mama would say. "And mine is a good boy," his mother might respond. I could not see that the two women would say anything else. I have always thought it was a mother's job to love her child even if nobody else could do it.

I thought of the time I finally left home, eighteen, without a place to go or any idea of what was waiting for me.

O N THE DAY I was leaving, Mama packed me lunch in a paper bag and gave me names and numbers of everybody she knew and trusted in the whole country.

"Where you think you'll go?" she asked, surprised when I had told her that I was going to get a bus ticket, that I was going to leave her.

"I don't know," I replied. "Maybe Florida," I added. "I could get a job at Disney World or something."

"Well, just make sure you wear your sunscreen," she noted, the sadness filling up her eyes. "Hackett women never did well in the sun." She stood at the bus station, watching the people come and go, all the travelers moving around us. She shook her head as if she couldn't believe that I was about to be one of them, one of those people leaving home.

"I'll come get you if you get homesick," she added.

I hugged her and took my suitcase from her. I could see that the bus was boarding. Once I found my seat, I turned around and watched her standing there by her car until she disappeared behind me. I was lost and found at the same time.

It turns out that I was gone for only a few weeks before she showed up to join me. We lived together until she met

Chance, an old widower who married her and brought her back to North Carolina. I stayed a while in Orlando by myself and then I followed them. Chance helped me get my own apartment and then I got the library job. He died a few years ago and Mama stayed in their house. We finally have some space between us, but sometimes I'm not sure we aren't still bound together in some unnatural way.

I thought about Lathin's mother. Since he hadn't seen her in ten years I wondered if she was even still alive, if he just told himself that she was in a home to grant himself a little comfort. Since I didn't really want to move into the messiness of my own maternal relationship, I figured I wouldn't ask him any more about that subject.

I settled in my makeshift bed and glanced at my watch. It was just after one in the morning.

FOUR

592.1

JELLYFISH

"What's it like?" I asked. "Being in there," I finished up the sentence, in case he didn't know what I was talking about.

I waited a while to ask him the question, but I had really wanted to know this from the first time we met. I was curious about such a place, wondered how it was to be in the inside of a prison, to be sent there, to belong there.

I had only been in a jail once. I was with my mother. I was maybe six or seven, not very old. I suppose it's something I'll never forget.

I guess that she was visiting some boyfriend who had gotten locked up. I don't know now who he was, but I know there was more than one who found himself in trouble.

We were in Fayetteville or Rocky Mount. Someplace we hadn't been for long. I can't recall the town.

Mama hadn't intended to bring me along, had mentioned it wasn't any place for a child, but there was nobody with whom I could stay and I had begged to join her. I thought of it as some kind of adventure.

"I'm just going to stay a minute," Mama said as we drove in the part of town I had never visited. "He owes us some money."

All of the parks gave way to parking lots as we drove into the center of the town. All of the buildings seemed cold and lifeless. We parked on the street and she held my hand until we were all the way inside. I knew Mama needed the money bad or she would have never gone to see this guy.

Once inside the building, she went up to the policeman seated behind a tall counter and asked about the man. Then she walked with me over to an area near the front door that was a little space for people to wait.

Mama headed with me to the far corner where I sat in a plastic chair with very strict instructions not to talk to anyone, not to move, not to leave, not to do anything but sit and wait. She glanced around nervously and then stuck her purse behind my seat, threw her coat around my shoulders, and walked back over to the counter. I watched her sign forms and exit through a long hall.

Her rules about my waiting on her, about sitting in one place and not talking to anyone, not moving, I recall thinking at the time, were simply too much to ask of a young girl, especially me. I ended up disobeying her within about ten minutes when I got up and walked over to the door. I even took a piece of gum from an old woman who told me she was there to visit her grandson. I thought there would be nothing wrong with that encounter.

The elderly woman came in after we did and she seemed harmless enough and I figured my mom wouldn't mind me talking to her. After all, I assumed Mama made the rule about not talking to anybody because she hadn't expected there to be a grandmother there. She would have altered her instructions if she had thought of that, if she had seen her first.

After the old woman handed me the gum, some policeman, one who seemed to know her, not the one behind the counter, came and told her she wouldn't be able to visit her grandson because he was in lockdown. He had said it without a bit of emotion, without a bit of regret for the old woman, as if it were something he said a hundred times a day.

I still remember how sad she looked. She shook her head, made that humming noise that old people make when they think a bad thing has happened. Then she handed me the whole pack of gum, Juicy Fruit, my favorite, and I took it from her and smiled.

"Thank you," I said and I chewed every stick waiting for Mama to come out. The old woman patted me on the head and nodded at me, but I knew she was just putting on a face. She was broken by something. Even as a child I could see that.

After she left, I sat and watched as the people went in and out the door Mama had gone through. I thought how they didn't seem very different from me or Mama or the grandmother who had given me gum and who had been sent home.

I guess since Mama had acted so nervous about leaving me in the waiting room, I had thought that people with family members in jail would somehow not be the same as us. I guess I thought they would look mean or bad or be marked up on the outside. But they all seemed just as nervous, just as out of place as Mama had.

I heard steel doors closing and counted four cameras on the walls and ceilings. I noticed the vending machines and thought I would ask for a quarter when Mama got back, thought I'd ask for a soda. I watched a little girl about my age and was just about to ask her if she wanted to play a game of I Spy. And then she left and I had to wait alone some more.

Mama didn't say much when she finally returned to the waiting room. She seemed resigned to something, that the relationship was over, I guess, or that she was never going to get her money, and it wasn't long before we moved again.

On our way home, Mama told me never to mention that trip to anybody. I guess she was worried what folks would say about her taking her child to jail. But it never really bothered me, and after meeting Lathin and thinking about prison, I remembered sitting in that waiting room, chewing Juicy Fruit gum and discovering that no matter where we are, we all pretty much look the same. That trip, however, was the closest I had ever come to life behind bars and I still wanted to know what it was like on the other side.

There was a moment before Lathin answered and I wasn't sure if he was still thinking about his mama and why she quit coming or if he was considering how to respond to my question.

"Probably a lot like falling into that dark place you talked about."

I recalled what I had said to him about my mental condition. And although I had no point of reference except for that twenty minutes in the waiting room at the county jail when I was just a child, I figured what he said must be true.

He decided to explain.

"You go in there thinking somebody made some mistake, that this really can't be happening to you, and soon as they understand that you ain't who they think you are, they'll let you out."

I wondered who people thought Lathin was, who he really was.

"You all the time calling your lawyer or talking to the guards telling them that you don't belong there and soon as your woman gets your money to the court, or the records get straightened out, you'll be so far gone from that place, they won't even recall what you looked like."

He paused, remembering how it was in the beginning for him, I suppose.

"You always wanting to know the lowdown on everybody else, but acting like you different, like you better or something."

I heard a slight laugh through the wall.

"And I 'spect you really believe it for a year or so. You

really think somebody made a mistake and somebody is going to come get you out, that somebody is working on your behalf and making it all right and one day you'd be laughing all the way out the gate and to the parking lot."

I wondered how he was sitting in his room, if he had made himself a bed like I had or if he was sitting up.

"I sure did."

I turned my face toward the wall trying to remember Lathin's eyes trying to recall what color they were, what shade of darkness.

"In just another day, maybe next week, most certainly by the winter, I'll be out of here."

I heard a sliding noise, made me think he was shaking his head and it was moving across the wall, like he couldn't believe his own story.

"You keep telling yourself, 'Can't no jailboss be interested in my little shit,' 'Can't no judge keep me under lock and key.' "

I remembered Lathin's face when I saw him at chapel.

"And all the other brothers just yessing you right along because they telling themselves the same stupid things."

I remembered his eyes being wide and not being brown, but more black, hard. I thought of how he glanced in my direction, how he seemed to know who I was as soon as he saw me.

"But another day comes, next week, fall then winter then spring, and your little ass is still in there."

He laughed, longer this time and haunting.

"So you turn into what you gotta be."

"What?" I asked, not following what he was saying. "What you gotta be?"

"A killer, a thief, a junkie, somebody's bitch, whatever they say you are. You become the thing they say."

I thought about what he was telling me.

"Why do you do that?"

"Just how it turns out."

Then he added, "That's how they keep the system going. Every day there's somebody reminding you why you're in there, what the policeman said you done, what the judge say it cost, what some white woman typed on that long roll of paper."

I thought about the court reporters, how I had seen them on television shows, sitting near the judge, how it seems they take notes all day. I wondered if they ever cared about what was going on or if they just recorded the conversations completely indifferent to the trouble being paraded before them.

"And it don't matter how you remember things, it's that piece of paper, that police report, that color jumpsuit you wearing, that number on your cell door, that begins to make you into the man they already decided you are."

I pulled the blanket up to my neck, trying to get warm despite the air conditioner blowing right in my face. It was cold sitting on the floor.

I considered Lathin's theory on criminal justice, wondering if that was why there was such a high rate of prisoners going back to jail after they get out. I knew that was a real issue for the justice system since I had helped a sociology professor work on his course about the lifetime criminal.

Lathin's idea seemed to make about as much sense as anybody else's notion. And maybe he knew best since he was a man on the inside.

" 'Course black men always wrestling with that," he added as if he had a lot more that he wanted to say.

"With what?" I asked, surprised with the direction he was taking our conversation, wondering if I had maybe missed something.

"That we are what the Man says we are. That slavery is still in our blood."

"Huh." I think I said out loud, not as a question, more as a way of noting I was listening.

"For black people in this country, that's what we know, what we've always known, and even though all the brothers and sisters like to pretend it's all way behind us, something from our grandpappies' lives, written in the history books, it ain't never gotten out of the stone-cold places in our hearts.

"It's still there, way down deep maybe, but still there. And as long as it's there, brothers always gonna wind up on the farm."

I turned away to glance at the ceiling. For the first time since staying at Holly Pines, I noticed that like the walls, it was also painted green, just not the same shade. I thought it was strange to use two different colors in the same room.

I guess the painters thought no one would notice, that since the residents were insane, we would miss the mistake.

And yet, it seems to me, after my time having psychiatric care, that crazy people notice that stuff even more, that we are fascinated with the details of life, the small things.

Lathin was still talking about his ideas about black men and why so many of them are in prison. I wasn't listening to everything he said and I knew there had been lots of books written about this very subject, that it was possible I could even tell him about some of what had been published, but I thought maybe I should just let him talk. After all, I was clear that I didn't know enough to give my own opinion.

He talked so much about it I imagined that he had thought through this a long time.

His voice trailed on.

"Underneath all the million-dollar contracts with rap stars and basketball players, it's there. Below all the NAACPing and minority representation, affirmative acting and Supreme Court justicing, it's there. Deep inside all of the hip-hop and drug-dealing and high educating and moving on up, we all still carry those trapped and shipped memories. We always know at some level that that's how we got to this country and that's how we stay."

Then he got sort of quiet and I couldn't hear what else he was saying even though I sensed it was just more of the same.

"You believe that?" I finally asked, wondering if he was just spouting out something he heard or if he had indeed worked through all of this processing himself.

"Like the Gospel, child."

I nodded. He was telling the truth, as far as I was

concerned. It did seem he really believed what he was confessing.

"Black men in prison because somewhere deep inside they minds, they remember the pull of steel around they ankles. They remember being chained up and penned like dogs. They remember being beat with whips and having collars on they necks and bits in they mouths. And one hundred and fifty years ain't gonna wipe away those kind of mind pictures."

He took a deep breath and went on.

"Getting hosed down with water so hard it blisters, sprayed for lice and fleas like mules, cuffed inside a metal box intending to break a stubborn streak, and being told when to piss, when to eat, and how to say 'Yes, sir' in that big-teeth, fancy-stepping way that makes your daddy loosen the grip on his Smith & Wesson and let us pass."

Lathin paused.

His voice had grown cold and distant like he was retelling a family secret that had been folded up and put away, like he was remembering something that he tried really hard to forget.

"Brothers in jail 'cause that's our oldest thought, our longest memory. And even though some of the others learned the Man's secret handshake and how to cut they eyes just right so as to make a little dough and live on Elm Street, send they children to private schools, you get them scared enough or high enough or desperate enough and they'll tell you the same thing, the same thing.

"They still hear they ancestors' bloody cries, still feel the butt of a rifle at the base of they cold neck, still pull at the air like they yanking cotton. They know. They remember. They just keep it small and far away."

A silence hung between us, a wall that separated us.

I wasn't sure of how to respond, so I just said what I thought, confessed to my ignorance.

"I guess I wouldn't know about any of that."

"No, white girl," he replied quickly. "I guess you wouldn't."

I rolled over on my side, closed my eyes, and wondered whether this huge gulf of unshared experience between us would keep us from any further conversation. I wondered if Lathin had gotten himself so worked up that he would choose not to say anything else to me, that he would suddenly remember that he was black and I was white and there was nothing to bring us together, nothing else to say.

It was quiet for a little while. A light breeze blew outside the window, a patient moaned in her sleep, and in that span of silence, that long, awkward break between me and Lathin, I found myself thinking about Terrell Chapman, the black boy I loved in seventh grade.

I had not thought of him in years, had not even thought of his name or what we had shared. As I lay on my side on the floor in my room at Holly Pines, I suddenly realized that he was the first boy I ever really cared about. I guess you would say that he was my first real love.

We were living in Swansboro, North Carolina, then. It's a little coastal town down near Camp Lejeune where Mama

followed some marine she had met when she worked at the
Waffle House in Burlington.

Bennie Jewel was the man's name. We lived with him almost four years until he got sent to Korea and we couldn't
go. That was the longest we lived anywhere and I thought
for a while that it might be where we settled, might turn
out to be a real home for us, a real community, which is
why I figure I let myself become interested in a boy.

Bennie Jewel was not a bad guy, not like some of the others we stayed with or that Mama brought home. He always
gave me little gifts, made me up my own room with pink cur-
tains and a matching bedspread. He seemed to care about me,
want to be a family with me. Even though I wasn't interested
in having a daddy at that point in my life, I didn't mind the
attention he was showing me. I sort of liked his attempt at a
relationship.

He gave me money every Saturday morning, an allowance,
when I cleaned up the trailer or shined his shoes, and he
was real respectful of Mama, really seemed to have deep
feelings for her, care about her, except when she made him
jealous.

Mama liked her men jealous, told me it kept them on
their toes. Of course, I saw the way they looked at her when
she flirted or carried on with a friend of theirs or somebody
at work. It was not what I would call a look of a man keeping on his toes.

I would call it more of a look of a man figuring out how
to keep his woman under control, a look that signaled

trouble for us when we got home. Getting her boyfriend jealous was not something I thought was ever good for a relationship, but Mama, telling me I was worrying about something I didn't know anything about, always acted like she knew what she was doing.

When Bennie got assigned to Korea, I think he and Mama wrote and called each other like they could wait through his overseas duty. There was this big night out together. There were roses and champagne at the house. I think he even bought her a ring, asked her to marry him, but Mama wasn't much on waiting.

Once his orders came through, I knew we wouldn't be staying there long, and sure enough, after Bennie left, Mama started looking through the maps she kept in a suitcase under the bed and we were there only about six months before she met another marine and we followed him to Norfolk. It was just the way of things for us. For her.

Before Bennie left and I thought we might live a while in Swansboro, I did enjoy a brief season of tenderness, though, a few months of what felt to me to be a normal life, the thing I had heard other girls talking about, but had never experienced on my own, falling in love.

Terrell Chapman was assigned to be my partner in science class. The teacher's name was Mr. Walters and he didn't really seem to like science. He was gone from the classroom a lot, down in the gym because he was the basketball coach, so the science partners spent most of the class working together on projects alone, trying to figure things out on our own.

Terrell was smarter than me. I knew this because I had

been in the school in sixth grade and I knew he had won two or three awards for making the highest grades on some tests. He looked so proud when he was called down from the bleachers in the gym. He wore a wide smile and glanced around to find his mother watching.

I could tell when Mr. Walters announced the partners that Terrell was disappointed that he hadn't been paired with Billy Myers or Coletta Causner, because the three of them were friends and they were all equally smart and they seemed to like to work together. Once he knew he was assigned to me, however, he didn't complain or treat me badly. He was real nice to me. So that after a couple of weeks, we found that we really liked each other and that we both had a natural disposition toward understanding invertebrates and the physiology of creatures that have no need for spines.

I think it surprised Terrell that I was as knowledgeable as I was since he had never noticed me before. Since I was always the new kid, I tried to keep a low profile in school. It was a way of managing the stress of starting over. I learned it was better not to be noticed than to set myself apart.

I never wanted to call attention to myself, give the other kids something to use against me, like making the best grade or becoming a teacher's pet, but I knew I was bright. I could tell that I had a grasp on learning that a lot of students my age didn't seem to have. I knew I remembered things read in a book or discussed in class better than a lot of kids. And if I liked a subject and if I was challenged, I could do real well on tests and papers.

Terrell and I would stay after school and work on our science projects or study for tests until way past supper time and the janitor would have to make us leave. He would walk me to the corner of the trailer park where Mama and I lived with Bennie, and we would stand at the driveway for a long time talking about my neighbors or laughing at one of his friends who would pass by on a bicycle and make some comment about us. We would stand there until a car would pull in and then he would say good-bye by sliding his fingers, ever so lightly, down the back of my arm as he handed me my books. It would sometimes make me blush.

I'd watch him as he turned back up the street and headed to the other side of the school, where I knew he would walk across the railroad tracks, and down a dirt road, where most of the black people in Swansboro lived.

We learned a lot about anatomy and scientific procedure that year. We learned about coelenterates and their single internal cavities. We learned about radial symmetry and circular body shapes with the skeletons on the outside.

We learned about the components of the nerve cells within the jellyfish that exist without any organized nervous system. How the membrane is thinner than a cobweb and how it decides what is allowed to enter and what is not. How it serves as a filter, an envelope of vigilance that protects the nucleus, the heart of the cell.

I learned how to drop my head back while he'd unbutton my shirt and slip his soft hand inside while lightly kissing the long line of my young neck. I'd move my fingers, like tentacles, along the inside of his thigh and tighten around the stiffness that grew in between his legs.

And we would study the magnitude of our trembles and how far we could get before one of us, usually me but sometimes him, would frighten and pull away, a layer of protection, thin as it was, that kept us from penetrating into the knowledge that was meant for more mature laboratory scientists.

"You tell your mama about us?" he asked me one day when we were inside Bennie Jewel's trailer.

We were alone because Mama and Bennie had gone off to see a movie in Jacksonville. They had left early that afternoon, wrote a note, and had it on the table when Terrell and I came home.

Mama had cooked pinto beans, had a bowl of it in the refrigerator with a little piece of cornbread on top. She had a cupcake next to the note. I handed it to Terrell.

"I told her about our science project," I answered, taking the cupcake from him and eating a bite from the other side.

Terrell smiled, wiped a bit of frosting off my lip.

"You tell your mama about me?" I asked, handing him back the snack.

He shook his head and his expression changed.

I didn't ask him why. At the time, I didn't think it was important. I knew my mother didn't care who I hung out with as long as he treated me nice and didn't take advantage of me. It wasn't because he was black that I didn't tell my mother he was my boyfriend. I just didn't want her asking me questions about him all the time, trying to find out how much I liked him, what we did together. As a young teenager, I gave my mother only as much information as the two of us could stand her having.

But after what Lathin had said, I realized that Terrell asked me the question because he was black and that he hadn't told his mother because I was white, that he understood that by being my boyfriend, he was breaking some very strict rule. He understood better than I what was and was not allowed in eastern North Carolina even as late as the 1980s.

When school let out for the summer, we were still going steady and I had expected that we would spend a lot more time together. We had made plans to go swimming. Bennie had promised that he would take us to the beach and we were going to find a few jellyfish, to study them up close, but it didn't work out that way.

Terrell took a job with his father harvesting cucumbers at a farm outside of town. I only saw him two or three times during all those hot weeks because he left early in the morning, Monday through Friday, returning after dark. I ended up working on the weekends, sweeping floors at the sewing factory where Mama had a third-shift job. The summer came and went and we had hardly been together at all.

When we started in the eighth grade, he was different. He was taller and stronger, but it was more than just physical changes. He bore a whipped look in his eyes, a breach of trust or snapping of innocence, both of which he tried to cover with bravado and teenage rage.

It was as if he hardly noticed me, dropped me without even telling me why. He started dating a girl who had moved into town over the summer. She lived with her grandmother, next door to Terrell, and she never seemed to like me.

It wasn't long before his grades fell and he was suspended when he took a swing at Mr. Collins, the football coach, an old white man who taught history. After that, I never saw Terrell again, since we ended up moving that winter. So many nights, however, I would lie in bed and try to understand what could have happened in a cucumber field that could steal away a boy's delight and make him grow a backbone that he hadn't needed before.

Hearing Lathin's words at Holly Pines made me realize that there are all sorts of things that I don't know, all sorts of equations I hadn't ever found myself in, made me realize that farms can grow more than ripe vegetables and sweet sun-kissed fruit and that prison yards spawn more than taut muscles and well-exercised hearts. Both of them can manifest evil in slow, subtle ways that tear away trust and apparently leave long scars that never really heal.

"What you scared of?"

His question surprised me since I thought he was angry for reasons I did and did not understand and that our conversation was finished. I had planned to get in my bed and go to sleep. I waited a minute before answering.

"Dying alone, I guess."

My head was down and I wasn't sure he heard me.

"And darkness." I lifted my voice. "I'm afraid of the dark."

"The dark?" he questioned, his voice sounding very surprised. "I miss the dark."

There was a long sigh.

"There's always a light on at the farm. Some big outside light shining in your window like the one outside ours now."

I looked up behind me at the light coming through. It was bright, but I thought manageable. I had never had any trouble sleeping because of it.

"A torture weapon like they used in Vietnam," he added, blowing out a long breath.

"Or the inside lockdown light that never goes off. Even in a storm, it's hooked up to a backup power supply."

He rolled over. I heard his body shift and land. I figured he was lying down like I was.

"Or a headlamp in your face waking you up in the middle of the night because some duty boy wants to have a little fun."

I turned on my side and repositioned the pillow.

"Burns the socket of your eyes, that light."

I slipped my hands between my knees.

"There's something real powerful about the darkness."

I wasn't sure what he meant. I never thought much about the power of darkness, only the fear of it.

"Like the cold, fertilized dirt where a seed starts to shake and stretch." His voice was turned away from the vent so that I had to strain to hear him.

"You know change never starts in the eye of the sun."
He stopped and cleared his throat and I listened for the explanation.

"It starts in the earth, the dark, dark earth. So that never
having darkness, never having the space to go deep inside,
never getting the opportunity to go down and come back
up, like the death of night and the homecoming surprise of
morning, well, it keeps a man ever thinking he can change
things about hisself."

I considered what he said as I followed the long bright
fingers of light that crept into my room.

"And not being able to change things." His voice became clear. "That's the beginning of the end for a brother
in prison."

The tree outside lowered its branches and the limbs
skirted the ground; the shadows twisted on the walls like
people in love.

"Sometimes, I pull the pillow over my eyes so tight, I almost smother just so I can have a little darkness."

I closed my eyes trying to see what it must be like to miss
darkness, but it came to no consequence. I'm always trying
to push the night away, illuminate all the corners, keep the
bulbs fresh in closets and attics, hide flashlights everywhere
I might need one, so that I'll never find myself faced with
that thick, closed expansion of blackness.

I wondered, as I heard about Lathin's grief at losing
darkness, if I found out that I would experience only light
for years and years, that I would never have darkness again,
if I would suddenly welcome it, embrace it, grieve to see it

go. And yet, even in the face of never knowing the dark again, I could not imagine such a turn of thoughts, such a dismantling of my fears.

I have been afraid of the dark for as long as I can remember. My fear is so old, in fact, I cannot even name when or how it all began. I only know that I learned it from my mother and that I have always slept with a night-light, a door cracked into a lighted hallway, or a lamp burning somewhere in my room. And the only times that I remember being forced into darkness, I emerged quite convinced that I had almost died.

My mother never explained how she came into such a fear. But it was because of her inability to cope with an absence of light that I learned how to be comfortable with my own inherited phobia. As I discovered how she learned to manage night—small lights in every outlet, flashlights in every drawer—her methods became mine in learning how to deal effectively with my fear.

When I was a child and we lost power because of weather or not paying the bills, we huddled together around the flame of a candle like two babies at their mother's breast. We dared not laugh too loud or move too quickly, as the tiny flicker could be extinguished and we would be left alone with our insatiable hunger for light and the worse-than-death consequences of darkness. And nights would go on forever as I learned to sleep with one eye open, weary that the candle would spill and burn and worried that my mother would wake to a darkened room.

Once, when I was about three, we rode up an elevator in

the hospital to visit an ailing friend of my mother's. It was the first time I had ever been in an elevator, and I was surprised at the tiny room that could take us up flights of stairs that we didn't have to climb. There were already three other people inside, having come up from the ground floor, and as we entered the small area and the doors closed, I remember the grip of my mother's hand, tight and sweaty. She had already noticed that there was only one small light overhead.

The light on the ceiling trembled as we rose a level and then simply went out, like a shooting star or radio music in the event of some emergency announcement. And even though the elevator was still moving, obviously still in working order, when the hard steel doors opened on the floor above where we had started, my mother fell out like she was pushed and then crawled into the nurses' station that was flooded in brightness.

She was so pale and so distraught, a doctor ran from a nearby patient's room and swept her up from the floor, but she would not be taken from the light. She would not go with him. She clung to the edge of that large wraparound desk and even though she was promised that she would not be left in the dark, she would not turn loose.

I stood there, in the corner, halfway between the daylight before me and the night from which we had both just come, and breathed in my mother's fear like a newborn takes in milk. I watched her and knew she was living out what would soon become mine. Her fear, like her pale skin and thin lips, would be passed on to me.

So I don't think that my fear sprang up from the happenings or circumstances of my own early years. I don't believe that I came about the fear because of my own personal experience or lived-out horror story. I think I loved and protected my mother so much that even at the early and holy year of three, I was taking in her pathologies just as I was taking in her applesauce and her love of trains. My mother was scared of the dark and then, just as if it were handed to me, like an order of what was to be, what was to come for me afterward, so was I.

Suddenly, the door at the end of the hall opened and closed, and footsteps came down the hall. I jumped up from the floor, onto the bed, and threw the blanket over me. I felt the glare of eyes from the door and heard the lock being twisted open and someone step inside.

My stomach tightened and I sensed the nearness of a body and the glow of a flashlight on my face. I did not open my eyes. I hoped whoever was on duty would not notice my sheets still lying on the floor. I waited to be questioned, trying not to appear alert or awake. I tried to steady my breathing.

Before too long, the light went out. And the person walked away and shut the door. The lock twisted. And then I heard them go next door and I wondered if Lathin was still lying on the floor or if he had gotten up and fallen on the bed too. But I dared not ask. I glanced around, relieved that the attendant hadn't said anything about the linens and pillow not being on the bed. I took in a deep breath and exhaled. I listened next door. I heard a conversation.

"Why aren't you in bed?" the attendant asked.

Although it was a man's voice, it didn't sound like Roy. I wondered who else was working the late shift and tried to recall whom I had seen earlier. I thought of Calvin, his kind smile and the way he often let us get away with things the other staff members wouldn't.

"Mattress is bad. I have to sit up," Lathin answered.

"Well, you need to get back in there," the voice replied softly.

I had seen Calvin in the cafeteria after chapel service. He only worked the weekends. He was quiet, didn't try to practice psychology on anybody, just got us from place to place, passed out medications, and often let us sleep a little longer or stay outside past curfew.

I heard sounds of a body moving and I figured Lathin was getting off the floor and into the bed.

"You need something to help you sleep?" Calvin asked.

"Whatcha got?" Lathin asked.

"Ambien, Tylenol PM, Thorazine, what's your favorite?"

I had never asked for sleeping pills and I was surprised to know they gave them out so easily.

"That first one," Lathin replied.

"Okay," Calvin responded. "I'll be right back."

I heard Lathin's door close and the footsteps trail down the hall. The hall door opened and fell shut.

"They been doing that every night?" I whispered the question, hoping that Calvin was out of range to hear me. I couldn't believe I never knew they came in with a flashlight and shined it in our faces.

"Guess so," he answered. "But remember I ain't been here long as you. You'd know better than I."

"Oh, right," I replied.

"I figure they have to check on everybody though, suicide watch and all."

"Yeah," I said. "I just didn't know they shined a light in your eyes," I added, thinking about what Lathin had said about darkness and the constant barrage of light in prison.

"You want to go to sleep?" I asked, thinking about his request for sleeping pills.

"Nah," he answered. "But you never know when something like that might come in handy."

I nodded even though he couldn't see me and I wondered if he would try to hoard pills for another attempt to kill himself. When I had that thought I wondered if I should get Calvin's attention and tell him what the prison inmate was doing, but when I heard the hall door open and the footsteps coming back down the hall I knew I wouldn't say a word. I knew I was too far into the night with Lathin to start breaking confidences. I heard the jangle of keys and the door next to mine unlock and open.

"Here," Calvin said, handing Lathin a pill, I figured.

There was a pause. Lathin must have taken the pill and was probably drinking water.

"Sleep tight," Calvin said as the door fell closed and I heard him lock it.

I waited until the footsteps stopped, the hall door opened and closed before I spoke. "You take it?" I asked.

He made a kind of snorting noise and I took that to

mean he hadn't, that he had found a way to hide the pill and pretend to Calvin that he had swallowed it.

Just like Lathin's memories of prison and his ideas about race and society, I realized there were a lot of things I didn't know and probably wasn't going to learn. I pulled the blanket off the bed again and threw it down on the floor once more.

I noticed the time on my watch again. It was two fifteen.

FIVE

070.4

JOURNALISM

"These are really small rooms, don't you think?" I looked at the four walls surrounding me.

"Bigger than what I'm used to." I heard him drop down. He was getting back to his position on the floor too.

"When you're in a prison cell, how do you keep from feeling like the walls are closing in on you?"

I studied the compact arrangement of the Holly Pines room, the four corners, up top and below at the floor. They seemed even tighter than they had earlier in my stay, and I couldn't imagine being stuck in anything smaller. I couldn't imagine being locked up in a tiny cell. I stood up and walked across the room. I walked end to end, corner to corner, and counted off the estimated dimensions.

"Oh, you just make it larger in your mind. Once you get locked up, you learn that lesson pretty quick in order to stay alive. You make things up for yourself. You pretend a lot."

"Hmm," I replied, not really paying attention. I was counting off the measurement. "Twelve by fifteen," I reported as I returned to the middle of the room, stopping just near the desk.

"What do you pretend about?" I asked, recalling what he had just said. And I wondered while he was in prison if he did as I had done when I first got sent to Holly Pines and decorated the room. I considered whether or not he used color, as I had, to block out the truth.

"I pretend the walls are the ocean, waves of blue saltwater. I think of them as being what steadies me, what holds me up."

I remained standing where I was. I was trying to understand what he was saying. I had never thought of walls as waves of ocean water.

He continued. "I pretend I am surrounded by the wide-open space that only seems like a cell because it is so safe. I make believe that if I had the desire I could dive down deep and long and come up on the other side of where I am or that I could swim to China if I wanted. But that I don't have to since I am perfectly at peace with all this blue around me and this slight bit of sky."

He stopped for a minute and I wondered where he had learned such a thing, who had taught him how to manage isolation and punishment so well. I thought about his image of the ocean, how he kept the walls from closing in on him by changing them into waves, and I considered the smooth glide of water against my skin, the easy way of drifting.

I closed my eyes as I stood in the center of the room,

trying to float, but the idea that I might drown in a dark current or be pulled down into the dismal mouth of some prehistoric sea monster jarred me back into the reality of where I really was. And the space was still narrow and scant. I glanced up. His fantasy was definitely not one that would work for me.

"How long did it take you before you really started to believe it?"

"Oh, I don't know."

I heard him shuffle about near the vent, trying to make himself comfortable, I figured. "A while, I guess."

"You start it the first time you got locked up?" I asked.

"Nah, it wasn't the first time. I wasn't smart enough then. I learned it later, I expect."

"How old were you the first time you were locked up?" I asked.

"About twenty. I probably stole something at the time. I don't recall what it was I did. I only remember that I was stuck in a place so small I couldn't even turn around without hitting a wall."

I felt my chest tighten. I cannot stand to be closed in.

"I was down South then. I had gone down there to visit a friend. Mississippi," he said. "I was in the wrong place at the wrong time, like a lot of my life."

"Was it the worst?" I asked, trying to imagine how many jail cells Lathin had stayed in.

"Nah, it wasn't the worst place," he answered.

I waited to see if he was going to tell me about the worst place, and he did.

"Worst place was Chicago. And I really was innocent that time. They picked up the wrong man for sure, but it didn't matter what I told them. They were convinced that I had murdered some guy on the South Side. And they picked me up and drove me downtown and they threw me in a box. A long steel box."

"How did you breathe?" I asked. I couldn't believe a man could live in a box, couldn't believe that our justice system would put a man in a box. There was so much I didn't know.

"There was a tiny hole above my head. I could see a little out of it too."

"Jesus," I responded.

"Yeah, I was calling on him too," Lathin replied.

"I would have died," I said. "Really, I would have died."

I have no power over my claustrophobia. I had known this a long time. Just hearing Lathin's story made me start to feel anxious. I walked around the room again.

"Nah, you wouldn't have died," he said. "You might pass out stuck in a box like that, but you won't die."

"Well, I would want to die," I said, standing at the far side, away from the wall we shared. "I wouldn't want to wake up and find myself still closed up like that. Yep, I think if I had the choice, I'd rather just die."

Lathin gave a short laugh. "You'd be surprised how much you want to live when you get close to dying," he said, sounding like a man who knew what he was talking about. "You'll fight to live even when you think death would be better."

"I don't know," I said, walking back. "Death's gotta give you more room than a steel box," I added. "It's got to."

Lathin didn't respond. I guess he was remembering being in Chicago and trying to decide if he wished he had died when he was there.

"You learn," he finally said. "You learn how to get by."

"Is that where you started thinking about the ocean?" I asked. I leaned against the wall and stepped on the tips of my toes, trying to feel how tall I could be.

"There was an old man somewhere close to me, in a box too. I guess they had a whole string of those things. I never could see who else was in the room, but I heard him. He kept me from going crazy, talking to me about the ocean, how big it was, how it could hold up anything."

I slid down to a sitting position. I could hear Lathin really well.

"I was pretty tore up," he confessed. "I reckon he knew it. I was crying pretty loud."

I nodded my head, forgetting that he could not see me respond.

"He hushed me, quoted Scriptures to me, promised me I wouldn't be there too much longer. Then he told me about the seawater and how to make it real in my mind." He hesitated a moment. "Guess you could say he saved my life."

"You ever see the old guy again, ever get to tell him thank you?" I asked, thinking Lathin had probably had lots of conversations like the one he and I were having, that he must have talked to lots of people between walls and bars and tops of boxes.

"No," he replied.

I listened to find out what happened, but Lathin never said any more about the man beside him. Maybe he didn't know, I thought, and I decided not to ask.

"Did it take you a long time to learn?" I asked.

"Learn what?" he asked. I guessed his mind had drifted.

"The thing about the ocean, the thing to keep from going crazy in small places?"

"Oh, that. It took a couple of months to get good at it, but you know, in prison you got nothing but time."

"Yeah," I said, as if I knew.

I got up and walked over to the other side of the room. I was still wanting to measure. I began to notice the items around me and I realized I hadn't seen the inside of his room. I figured they were alike, but I thought I would ask to be sure.

"Is your desk under the window or by the sink?"

"By the sink," he replied.

"And the cabinets under the sink, are they locked like mine?"

I pulled at the small doors, but they wouldn't open. I had tried them before when I first got in the room. I had wanted a place to put my brush and comb. I was surprised to discover they were locked.

"Don't know," he replied.

"Your desk got drawers?"

I was suddenly surprised at how wide-awake I felt. Somehow in the discussion about boxes and oceans, I had gotten my second wind. I felt as if I could talk all night. I wanted to learn as much as I could about Lathin, about prison life, about the room at the end of the hall.

"Looks like it," he said.

And then I realized that he was answering my questions as if he were guessing. All of a sudden, I understood that he wasn't walking around like I was and that he probably wasn't even able to, that he had been stuck in one place the whole time we had been talking.

"You chained?" I asked, wondering what it was like for him, wondering why they wouldn't let him have a little freedom in a locked room.

He mumbled something but I really couldn't make out his response.

I sat down at the desk, in the chair, my back to our wall. I stared at the other wall in front of me.

"Why do they handcuff you?"

"Reckon to keep me from breaking glass or climbing out the window."

"Would you do that?" I turned in the chair to face his voice.

"Don't know," he replied. And then he added, "Maybe."

"Yeah, me too," I said softly. And then I added, "I mean, if I knew I was going back to prison."

I leaned the chair behind me so that it rested on the back two legs. I thought about how Charlie was always having me speak to the students who did that in the library. He said it was a safety hazard and that the library could be sued if somebody hurt themselves.

I usually let them sit like that anyway. I hated spoiling

anybody's fun. And most of the time it was how the students sat to think better. I could see them concentrating, leaning back, their brows knitted in thought. They weren't causing any trouble. And I didn't see ruining their library experience. I never was one for being punitive.

As I sat in that position on that night, I realized how good it seemed to sit that way. I discovered that I loved how it felt letting my feet dangle off the floor. I found it to be comfortable and suddenly understood why so many people like to sit like that. It was a good way to think.

I wrapped my ankles around the bottoms of the legs and dropped my head back. I saw old water stains on the ceiling, large brown circles that had been painted over but not concealed.

"How would you get away?"

I snapped my head forward, awaiting his answer, and it threw the chair down on all fours. There was a loud bang. I worried that the noise might bring the attendant back. So I drew in my breath and held it. I wasn't sure if I should hurry back to my bed or just stay where I was. Since having checked in at Holly Pines, I had never been awake or made any loud noise at that time in the morning.

Lathin waited a few seconds too. I figured that he must have been worrying about the same thing. I heard nothing from next door.

I was quiet for a few minutes and then recalled what I had asked. I thought about the sleeping pill he had been given and considered that maybe if he was going to escape, he had plans to break the pill up and slip it in a guard's drink. I found the idea quite exciting and believable. I had, after all, in fits of weakness, read a number of thrillers and mysteries. I didn't tell most of the others at the library, since they only read fiction from the literary section.

"Even though it's tall and barred, the window looks like the best out," he said.

I glanced over at my window. I hadn't really studied it before and I looked at it in a different way this time.

The steel bars were rusted, but still appeared like they would be difficult to get through. They were thick, not something a person could bend or work through them. They appeared to be attached at the top and bottom and sides with big bolts. "Can't file through them," I responded and got up to take a closer look.

I stood underneath the window. I could see how the bars were installed. "They're only screwed in at the sides. They aren't welded or cemented in." I was surprised to see that on close examination, the window was not very secure. I figured I could move the bars.

I walked back to the desk and got the chair. Then I slid it over. I stood on it and I pulled at the bars and felt how they seemed a little loose.

"With a screwdriver you could certainly detach them from the wall." I stood on my toes trying to feel at the top. They were not drilled into anything. Yanking them out was definitely something that could be done with the right equipment and enough time.

"You got a screwdriver?" Lathin sounded sarcastic.

"No," I said in response like I was talking to an old

friend. "They took my tool chest away from me when I checked in."

He made a snort. I think he thought I was funny.

"But," I said, feeling excited and recalling what I had in my possession, "I do have a very strong ink pen."

I jumped off my chair and went over to my desk to find it. I moved things around, not being able to locate it. Finally, I flipped through the pages of my journal and found it in between my last entries.

I held it up and considered the possibilities of whether or not it could serve as a screwdriver. It was a big pen, one that I had been given as a gift from some coworker. It was the kind that uses refills, a screw top with a pocket clip on the side. The design on both ends looked like a giant spiderweb and I always liked the pen because it fit really well in my hand.

I pulled it apart, studied all the parts to it, and then put it back together again. I walked to the vent behind the bed through which we had been talking, and, still holding the pen, I knelt down and examined the opening between us.

"Now, how do I get it to you?" I said this as much to myself as to Lathin. I glanced around the room trying to see if there was any other connector between us. There was nothing else. It would have to be exchanged through the vent.

"Do you think if I put it in the vent you could get it?"

I slid my fingers around the vent cover and found that it was merely pushed in, like the top of a cardboard box. I pulled it out easily and peered inside. I could see through the slants of the adjoining cover and into Lathin's room. There was merely one long metal duct separating us.

I heard him move around a bit and then pull on the cover on his side. There was a bang and I knew he had slid his cover out as well. I threw the pen toward him and it made a loud rattle as it fell inside.

Suddenly, the outside door down the hall opened and closed. I hurried to put the cover on the vent on my side. The footsteps were close and clipped, and in my quick attempt to replace the cover I worried that Lathin would not be able to close up his side in time. I snapped it in place and jumped in the bed, quickly leaning over to pull the blanket and pillow just before the key entered the lock and my door fell open.

"What's going on down here?" the voice behind the flashlight inquired. It was a voice of suspicion. The attendant was obviously curious and a bit annoyed. He had just had to come down here to give Lathin a sleeping pill. I guess there were other things he wanted to do during that shift than check on the patients.

"Calvin, is that you?" I asked as I sat up, trying to appear as if I had just been awakened. I rubbed my eyes, playing the part of the sleepy patient as well as I could.

"Yeah, it's me," he answered abruptly, sounding as if he didn't believe my act.

He shined the light around the room. He stopped at the chair that was pulled away from the desk and sitting under the window. He walked inside the room. "You watching for something outside?" He turned on the overhead light and headed toward the far side of the room. He was examining the window.

"No," I replied and then I heard Lathin trying to put his vent cover on. It was a bit too loud. I was sure that Calvin could hear him. I coughed to hide the noise. Lathin was apparently having more difficulty than I did. He kept pushing and I kept coughing, being as loud as I possibly could.

Calvin turned in my direction away from the window. I sputtered some more.

"Do you think I could have a glass of water?" I asked between coughs. I kept making as much noise as I could. I hurt my throat coughing so hard.

"Yeah, but first let me check on something." Calvin made his way to the door. He had heard Lathin. I knew that I had to think of something.

I threw aside my blanket on the bed and fell forward. I coughed even harder. "I think I really need it now," I said as dramatically as I could. I knew my face was flushed. I knew I looked like I was in peril.

Calvin glanced at me and then at the door. He sighed, like I was a real bother to him, like he knew he was being played, but he went over to the sink, unlocked the cabinet, and got out a plastic cup. He turned on the faucet and filled the cup with water, turned off the faucet, and brought it over to me. I drank it slowly until I didn't hear anything next door.

"Thank you," I said.

I kept taking sips and once all the water was gone, I

wiped my mouth. I coughed once more, just for verification that I really had needed the water and then I handed him the cup, and lay my head on the pillow.

"Now, what were you doing in here?" I asked very calmly. I surprised myself at how easily I had taken to the art of deception.

He threw the cup away and headed to the door. "A noise," he said. "I heard a noise."

"Oh, it was probably the tree," I said, lying. "There's a limb beating against the window, been doing it all night."

He turned off the overhead light and shined his flashlight at the window.

"Is there a storm?" I asked, trying to make conversation, trying to give Lathin a little more time to get in the position he needed to be in, trying to sound innocent to Calvin.

"Just a late summer wind," he answered, sounding like a poet. Then he lit up the corner where the vent was. He paused, but didn't say anything. And then he shut the door and walked down the hall. He didn't even go to Lathin's room. I heard the hall door as he walked through it. I heard it as it closed.

"Wow! That was a close one." I got up from the bed. Once again I threw the blanket onto the floor. I felt excited. "What do you think they'd do to me if they thought I was helping you escape?" I felt my heart race. I hadn't ever been involved in such a crime before. I suddenly enjoyed the feeling of breaking rules.

Lathin didn't respond.

"Hey, you all right?" I thought it was odd that he was

being so quiet. Then I got worried about him. I edged closer to the vent.

"Yeah," he said, "just trying to get back to my spot." I heard him moving around. I wondered how he was managing to get up and down off the bed so much if he was handcuffed or chained.

"Did you get the pen? Do you think it will work?"

I heard him snap the vent cover on.

"Nah, I can't reach it. I think maybe it fell in between a joint or at the collar."

"Yeah?" I asked. "Maybe I can get it and try again."

"*No!*" Lathin sounded mad. "Just leave it alone!" Then his voice quieted down. He tried to sound comforting or reassuring. "I don't want him coming back," he explained.

I stood up, my feet at the vent.

"He's already suspicious enough."

"Okay," I said, feeling a little hurt that he wasn't at least interested in my escape plan. I waited a minute or so and then I slid my weight down against the wall. It was hard and cold, like it had felt in the beginning of the night. I assumed the best of the night was over, that all the excitement and noise had exhausted Lathin. I wondered how long it would be before I fell asleep. I closed my eyes to try and relax.

"Why don't you tell me about your life?"

His question surprised me. By that time, I thought about just telling him good night and putting my linens on the bed and going to sleep. Relaxed, my second wind had come and gone. But then I didn't. I thought that the conversation, even though it had turned in a different direction when Calvin interrupted us, was still the best discussion I had had since being at Holly Pines. I decided to keep talking. I answered his question and the night wore on.

"What about my life?" I replied. A question to his question.

"I don't know, anything."

I pulled the blanket around me as I sat wedged between the bed and the vent.

"It's boring."

"Can't be," he replied.

"And why can't it? I've lived it. I ought to know."

"It's a life, ain't it?"

His voice was close to the vent. It sounded as if he was lying with his face toward me.

"Yeah, it's a life," I said.

"Then it can't be boring. Days can be boring. Weeks can be boring. A relationship can be boring, but a whole life?"

I didn't know if he was asking or telling.

"A life cannot be boring," he added.

I guess he was telling.

"Okay, then," I responded. "I'll tell you about my life and afterwards you may just eat those words."

"All right, lay it on me."

I didn't know where to start. I mean, how does one tell about one's life? I wondered. What should I start with? I considered where to begin, pausing a few minutes, and then I thought about my mother. I thought I would start with her.

"My mama didn't know she was pregnant with me until she was almost seven months along. I guess she never had, what you'd call normal periods. Otherwise, she'd have known." I waited for him to say something, but he didn't.

"Anyway, right after I was born, we moved from near Raleigh, North Carolina, where Mama's from to Orange County. Guess she was looking for something colorful they didn't have at home."

I had never thought of this before.

"I think we stayed there until I was two or three and then we moved to Rose Hill, Kinston, Rocky Mount, Burgaw, Fayetteville, Burlington, Swansboro, Norfolk, Clayton, and finally Greenville." I counted the towns on my fingers.

"Mama worked as a waitress in most of those towns, usually at Waffle Houses or pancake places, late-night shifts usually. She likes breakfast," I added. "She was a seamstress in an underwear mill, an assembly line worker at some paper company, a housekeeper at Howard Johnson's, and a cashier at the automatic car wash. Best I could tell, she was good at all of her jobs, but I doubt she was ever happy at any of them."

"What she want, to stay at home and keep you? Cook fancy dinners and play card games with you when you got home from school? Have your daddy around?"

"No, I don't think that was it."

I thought about the community college courses she would start but never finish, the way she'd get all dressed up to go for an interview at the business offices downtown, but then never go in.

"I think she wanted to be a newspaper reporter."

Lathin made a noise like he was surprised.

"She kept all these newspapers around, had subscriptions

to lots of them. They were always the first bills she'd pay, even before the rent or electricity. But she'd read them, especially the feature articles about people in the community or the editorials, and she'd say stuff like 'Hell, I can write better than that,' or 'Why would they print that lousy story?' "

I stopped, remembering the countless times she'd call reporters to criticize their work or make corrections, the extra pair of scissors that she bought and kept on all the tables in our trailer or apartment to cut out the articles she especially liked or hated, and the folded-up one that she had in the zippered compartment of her wallet next to the picture of me and her together when I won an award for Perfect Attendance when I was in kindergarten.

I decided to tell Lathin about it.

"She wrote the editor one time when we lived in Fayetteville. It was something in response to a story on dangerous women drivers. And it really made her mad."

I recalled how she went on and on about that editorial, how she finally decided to respond. She had gone to the store and bought a new pen and pad of paper. I would never forget that letter. She must have read it to me a hundred times before she ever sent it.

"After working on it at least three days, she finally got it like she wanted it. And it went,

" '*Dear Editor,*

" '*As a female driver I was especially displeased with your story dated August 12, 1975. The careless and undocumented way in which this story was researched and writ-*

ten leads me to respond to several of Mr. John B. Allen's dubious allegations. Number 1: Women are not the driving force behind the overall increase in rates of insurance. In fact, according to recent statistics, MEN,'

"And this was in bold capital letters," I said as a sidebar to Lathin.

" 'AGES 18-24 HAVE THE HIGHEST RATE OF ACCIDENTS, HIGHER THAN ANY GENDER OR AGE GROUP. *It is this youthful male category which raises insurance costs for everyone and not the driving records of women of any age. Number 2: Yes, women are sometimes seen putting on makeup while driving or trying to discipline children sitting in the backseat, but this is not to be considered a driving hazard since all of the women I know learned at a very early age how to do more than one thing at a time. And I will add, if men would assist them in some of the duties for which women have to care, perhaps we could drive with a complete focus on the road.*

" '*And finally, Number 3: If you're really so worried about your teenage daughter learning to drive, maybe you should remember the fact that more girls are injured or killed sitting on the passenger's side of the car than those who are driving.*'

"And it was signed, 'Respectfully submitted, Ms. Belle Lucille Hackett.'"

I drew in a deep breath, tired from my recitation. I hadn't quoted it out loud to anybody before. It was a long editorial. If I remember correctly, it had been edited, shortened for space purposes. Mama had told me that too.

"Why you memorize your mama's letter?"

"It was like some passage in the Bible to her. She kept it in her pocketbook and must have pulled it out and showed it to me eight or ten times a week. I learned how to read from that newspaper clipping."

"She wrote a good letter," he said.

"Yep," I replied. "But that was the only one." I stood up and got the plastic cup out of the trash can where Calvin had thrown it when he was in my room before. I turned on the faucet and got a drink of water.

"I guess it's like Mary and her little dress that hung in the closet, my mama never had the courage to try on the possibility that she might in fact be able to write a stupid article."

I walked over to the corner and sat down. "So she poured coffee and scrubbed toilets, stitched lace on panties, and gave out change, but she never tried the thing she loved. She never wrote a newspaper story."

There was a pause before he spoke.

"You like her?"

"What do you mean?"

"I mean are you like her? Do you have some idea of yourself wadded up in the corner of your billfold? Some busted dream you don't tell nobody else about?"

I drank a swallow of the water, starting to feel a tiny bit defensive.

"Or you just keep hers like it was yours too?"

His question surprised me.

"I'm a librarian," I answered, sounding a bit more proud than was probably necessary. "Over at the college."

"Yeah?" It wasn't what he asked.

"Well, I don't know," I responded. "I haven't ever thought about it."

I sat in the quiet of that little psychiatric hospital room surrounded by empty walls and a meager space for reflection and thought hard about what I loved, what I would choose to do if I could, what career or job or avocation I might decide upon if all the choices were available. It was a bit surprising that I had never had those thoughts before. I simply did what had to be done. I paid my bills. I lived a quiet life. I worked.

I thought about how my life might be different if eight years earlier I had not been standing over near the checkout line to get on a computer when Charlie came by on his way to Human Resources with a written request for another staff librarian. If he hadn't said out loud to the woman behind the desk, "I've got to run this up to Personnel." And then he added, "I can't believe you want to live in California."

And if she hadn't rolled her eyes and waved him off and then seen the want ads folded under my arm and said, "You looking for a job, honey?" Like she knew me. Like she knew I was meant to take over her position. I wonder how things might have been changed if that simple and unplanned meeting in the library with the departing librarian hadn't occurred on that particular day, if I hadn't taken the apartment Chance and Mama offered me, if I had stayed in

Orlando and tried to make it work with the delivery guy I had started dating. Mark was his name and he wanted to buy a boat and sail to the Bahamas. We both liked coffee ice cream, but didn't have much else in common than that.

"When I was six I took four ballet lessons. They were free as an incentive to get parents to pay for a year's worth. Of course, Mama didn't. In fact, we moved right after the fourth one. But God, I loved those lessons."

I drank the last bit of water and put the cup down beside me. I wondered why I had suddenly decided to tell that memory. I was still thinking about Mark and the way he made a slight clucking noise, his eyes dancing with life, when he slid his hand across the side of a boat. "N-i-c-e," he would say, drawing out the word for more than a few beats. I was usually bored by him when we were together.

"They were in a lady's house, downstairs. She had a big basement, made it into a dance studio. And she said I was good, claimed I had natural talent."

I smiled, remembering the long elegant lines Miss LaVelle made as she leaned over the bar showing us how to reach for something way beyond us. She was as pretty as a flower and I thought about the soft pink way she felt and how she lifted my leg behind me, how I twirled one day after everyone else had left.

Arms stretched out to my sides, standing on my tiptoes, a piano playing, just twirling and spinning, in my own little world, thinking I would never stop. I thought about my cousin PeeDee and how she had laughed when I showed her that summer after my lessons, how she had wanted me to teach her too. I thought about how we had danced together.

One time we danced at the edge of a field. It was late in the morning, the sun was white-hot, already high in the sky. We had snuck away from doing our chores and we ran over to where the neighbor had parked his truck. He had left his door open and the radio was playing. He had walked to the other end of the field; we could see him down there talking to a worker on a tractor. He turned in our direction, since we were standing near his truck. I had told her that we should go back to the house, that he might think we were messing around in his stuff, but PeeDee wanted to stay where we were. She was listening to the music.

"Dance!" she shouted at me.

I waved her off as I turned to walk away. "Let's go!" I yelled back, trying to get her to follow me.

"Andy, listen to the song, dance with me!" she said again and started swaying back and forth to some country song that was playing.

I glanced down at the end of the field. I could see the farmer starting to move in our direction and then I looked back at PeeDee. She had jumped in the back of the truck. And she was so beautiful, so carefree. The farmer was only a couple hundred yards away, but PeeDee always had that way of talking me into everything. So, I jumped up there with her and I took her by the hands and we twirled around in that old truck bed, laughing and dancing until the song ended. We jumped off and ran away just before the old farmer got to the truck.

I shook the memories from my mind. They were of no value to me then. I was surprised I even thought of those four lessons or that dance in the field with my cousin. It was silly to have brought it up to Lathin.

"I was just a little girl when I took the classes. There's never any way I could have made it as a ballerina."

I picked up the cup and then crushed it in my hand.

Lathin didn't respond.

"Did you know that the average weight of a ballerina in New York is one hundred and two pounds?"

I threw the cup toward the trash can. It floated only a few feet and fell to the floor. I was mad that I remembered the dancing, mad that I had, at one time, thought being a dancer was actually possible.

"I haven't weighed less than one hundred and fifteen since I was fourteen years old." I pulled at the inch of fat hanging over my pants. And then I added, "And the average dancing life span for a ballerina is only seven to ten years, and that's only if there aren't any injuries."

I fluffed up the blanket around me. "So see, even if I had been a dancer, my career would be over now anyway."

I thought again about Miss LaVelle, wondered if she was still teaching or if she quit having anything to do with that work. She was so graceful, so full of goodness. She was so beautiful when she moved to the music, tilting back her head and smiling every time she turned and bowed.

I wanted to be just like her.

"What happens to the old dancers?" Lathin sounded like he was far from his bed, somewhere away from the vent.

Since I figured he was chained to the bed, I assumed he had just moved way to the other side. I did hear him well enough to know what he asked, though, and I realized that I had never really heard that question raised before. I pondered it before I responded.

"They teach, I suppose, or become presidents of art councils or something. They judge beauty pageants or . . . I don't know." I shrugged.

"A dancer probably never imagines what happens when they can't dance anymore, so I suppose that they're likely good candidates for being in a place like this for a while."

And then I considered that it must be very difficult, giving up a lifetime of pleasure, of having your body do what it did for so long and then suddenly finding arthritis and joint injuries keeping you from the stage. I figured facing old age for them is harder than for most.

"So, you might have ended up here anyway."

"Yeah." I smiled, thinking that was funny, thinking he was right.

" 'Cept they can always dance," he said, startling me. He sounded as if he gotten closer. I guess he had turned over in the bed and was facing me again.

"Make no money for it, maybe, have to give up their position in some ballet company, but even if they're old, they ain't like ballplayers who can't play ball no more. A person can always dance."

"Yeah, I guess there's always that."

I recalled Miss LaVelle explaining how even if she was in a wreck and paralyzed that she would never stop dancing, that even if her arms and legs couldn't move, she was sure the music could never betray her, that it would always lift them in rhythm.

"And they know they did it. There's that too," he added.

I didn't say anything in response. I felt as if he were goading me into some conversation I wasn't interested in having.

"So that's it then, the thing you love?"

"Yep," I said like a teenager, finished with answering the parental questions. "To dance." I waited and then decided to add, "I mean, if all things were like I could choose."

"What you mean by that?"

"What?" I asked, not understanding his question.

" 'Like I could choose'?" He repeated what I had just said to him. "What you mean by that?"

"I mean I couldn't choose then because we didn't have the money for more lessons and I can't choose now because I'm too old."

He made a noise like he was mocking me.

"Well, I didn't have any choice. I only had four lessons, and Mama couldn't afford to pay." I felt like I was talking to somebody who had no idea about what he was saying.

I explained in my most reasonable voice. "And it's silly to think about it now. I'm too old. Most dancers have been training since they were old enough to walk. A person can't just up and decide they want to be a ballerina."

Lathin made another noise, like a snort or a laugh. It was true, he was mocking me.

I turned around and faced the wall. I felt angry that he was even implying such a thing. And even though he really hadn't made such an implication, I knew what he was getting at, and I felt mad that he was making me defend such a universal truth as the fact that a thirty-something-year-old can't up and decide to be a dancer. I didn't respond.

"So your mama keeps an old piece of paper that has her name printed on it from years and years ago and you have some memory of a little bitty self that danced four times in somebody's basement and fell in love with dancing; and that's all you claim to have? That's all you claim to get to choose?"

"No, I didn't say that. I know I have choices. Choices about what I'll eat for supper, what I'll wear to work, my friends—"

He interrupted me. "But you ain't got no choice about the thing you love?"

He said it with spite and I shut up. I knew I wasn't going to fight with him. I have never been one to argue.

"Well?"

He waited.

"Oh, now I made you mad?"

I didn't say anything.

"That it, then?"

I felt him near, but I was still not going to talk just yet.

He took a deep breath like he was inhaling smoke and then he told me this story.

It was three twenty-five in the morning.

55 1.45

ESERTS

"My mama got a plant when she was a teenager."

I was curious to see how a story about his mother was going to change what had happened between us. I was curious to hear what he was going to share. I waited.

"She bought it from some man traveling on the train coming from out west. He had a suitcase full of 'em, dug up from the desert I guess, and he sold them to people for a penny apiece. They were funny-looking things. Cactus, it was called. You heard of 'em?"

I still wasn't speaking to him, but I certainly knew about cacti. I had studied the reading list for a botany class at the college. Since being a partner with Terrell, I had always been interested in science.

Because of my studies, I knew there were more than a few species of cacti and even though I had never kept any myself, I knew that they were an interesting variety of plant.

I recalled reading that they flourished in drought and they root extensively and usually quite shallow so as to absorb every bit of moisture that lands near them. I knew they were, of course, native to the desert, both high and low, and that it was difficult to keep them alive and growing if you take them out of their natural habitat. I recalled that their skin was like wax and that they plump up as a way to hold rain.

"Well, back then they was a rare thing. And all the other people who got one when she got hers killed theirs. Didn't know how to take care of it."

I could imagine how people who didn't live in the desert could sabotage a cactus.

"Gave it too much water, put it someplace it would get too much shade, kept the soil too fertilized or, like people will do, just pulled it apart trying to see inside it. None of 'em lasted more than a couple of weeks."

He waited.

" 'Cept Mama's."

I pulled my legs up and wrapped my arms around my knees. I thought about the tenderness required to care for such a thorny, prickly plant, figured that was the reason I had never kept one. I was not very patient with houseplants. I suddenly thought of the couple I had at home, African violets, and I hoped Mrs. Bishop had remembered to water them.

"She babied that thing like it was a pet dog or something. Sang to it, read to it. Hurried home from her work to check on it. She worried over that thing like it was some special gift from Jesus, brought down for her gentleness alone."

I smiled. I knew that kind of devotion.

"She had it before any of us were born, and she acted like it was part of the family. We all grew up knowing how to say 'Thank you,' and 'Yes, sir,' and 'No, ma'am,' and how to be careful with that plant."

He stopped.

I figured he was remembering how it was when he was a boy, the things he learned, the rules he obeyed.

"Anyway, she kept the thing in a red clay pot out on the porch in the summer, up front where the sun was the hottest."

I nodded. She had put it in the appropriate place. She must have known that they were used to a lot of sunlight.

"I always thought for sure that thing would shrivel from the heat, but it didn't. It would turn a lighter shade of green, but it didn't wither and rot like some of the other ones she kept out there."

I was about to respond that she had done the right thing, but I didn't. I just listened.

"Then she would move it inside the kitchen next to the woodstove when it got cold. She'd eat her dinner and always be looking at it out of the corner of her eye, and don't even ask me about what she said to us about touching it."

He made a kind of humming noise.

"She dared us children to break a stem or stick our fingers in the dirt."

I dropped my chin to my knees.

"Worse whipping I ever got was when I came in the house and bounced a ball too close to that damn plant and made it slide off its saucer."

He exhaled a long, deep breath, thinking about his punishment, I suppose.

"For more than ten years she tended to that thing. Gave it more attention than she did to us children or the garden or any of her church friends."

I raised up to hear what he was saying. I sensed this was important and I didn't want to miss a thing.

"She watered it only on holidays. It became part of the celebration. She'd wipe down the pot, blow over those long spiny arms, like she thought her breath would make them stretch for her. Then she'd pour just a little water from her favorite drinking cup onto the soil. I swear she even put on her best dress when she did it."

I couldn't help myself, I laughed.

"I thought it was because it was Independence Day or May Day that she put on something new, but after a while, I realized she was just dressing up to feed that plant."

I shook my head. The relationship Lathin's mother was having with a plant was starting to sound a little crazy.

"Then one day, a November day, I believe, it was cold I remember. I had gone to school, come home for lunch. And the plant was inside."

I heard him shift at the vent.

"And all of a sudden, a small yellow puff, a swollen husk, started to grow from one of the limbs. And two days later another one grew. They weren't no bigger than the tip of your little finger."

I stuck out my pinkie to measure how big he was saying.

"But then, this other one started to sprout, down from underneath one of the arms, on the other side. And while the other two buds quit growing, this one got bigger and bigger until it was as big as a man's fist."

I folded my fingers in a tight ball, examining the size of my hand, wondering how it compared to the bud he had seen.

"Mama was so excited she brought in everybody she knew to see if they could tell what was going to happen to these little tight mouths of skin. She brought over neighbors and the men who were known for how they could grow things."

Lathin's mother reminded me of myself in the library when I was looking for something. I liked to involve a lot of other folks too.

He continued. "She even got a white farmer to come in our place to look at it. And trust me, that didn't happen unless they was there to get money or blood."

He said this, I could tell, going outside the story just for me.

"She had told him that it was such an unusual thing that he might want to grow them instead of cotton, that maybe he could make a lot of money with them."

I found myself enjoying his story.

"The farmer studied it for a little while, but he didn't know what it was or what it was going to do either. And after he remembered where he was and then saw us children standing around watching, he suddenly looked like he was in a real hurry to leave. He acted like he was standing in shit or something."

Lathin made a funny noise.

Since there was a pause in the conversation, I thought about stopping him to tell him about the star cactus. I was pretty sure this was the kind of plant his mother was growing. I considered explaining how they can lie dormant for years and then suddenly burst into a yellow star for just a couple of hours or a day and then fold back into themselves.

I wanted to let him know that I had helped a botany student write a term paper on desert life, how we had researched together the genuses and species of succulents. But I refrained. It wasn't really all that important or interesting and I figured, since he was telling this story, he already knew about the flowering habits of star cacti by now anyway.

"We watched that thing for three weeks. Mama tenderly adding dirt to the pot, setting it in the window for the morning sun, moving it to the kitchen for the late shine."

I settled down beside the wall.

"I swear that she was more worked up over that fist opening than she was about the Second Coming of Christ."

It certainly sounded like she was highly invested in that plant and I sat and thought that I understood how that could happen. It made perfect sense to me that a woman could get so tied up in the matters of a plant, especially if she was feeling lost and hopeless in the other parts of her life.

I remember Grandma telling me something before she died, trying to help me grow up, trying to help me live with truth. "You can't lay hold of everything that comes into and out of your life," she said. I guess I was fourteen or fifteen. It was before I got pregnant and after I stopped going to her house for the summers. I was staying with her for a weekend while Mama was off with some serviceman. We had just fixed a kettle of water for tea and had gone out to the front porch. I watched as she moved out the screen door and I could see then that she was getting old. Her back was hunched over and her fingers were gnarled and bent. She held the door open as I walked through, carrying our cups.

"Some things you got to let just come and go. Just come and go," she said again. The door swinging closed behind me.

Grandma often repeated herself, like a call-and-response from church.

"Settle your mind on those things you can make sense of," she said as she took her tea.

We made our way to her rocking chairs and sat down. The sun was setting and there was nobody else around. I was not myself at the time and she could tell I was at a place in my life where I was in need of help. I felt a slight breeze coming from the north, a sure sign of a storm, she used to say, and I had wrapped my arms around myself, taking slow sips from my cup of tea.

Grandma had been watching me. "If you dwell on the things that overwhelm you, you'll get swept away as sure as if you were dust on a walking path. Think on the small things, Andreas," she said. "Think on them." We rocked while the storm poured in.

I had not thought of that conversation in years.

Lathin was still talking. I was afraid I had missed an important part of the story, but I could soon tell that I hadn't gotten too far behind.

"She didn't even leave the house on the weekends because she was so afraid that she would miss the blooming."

I turned my head to rest on the left side so that I could see out the window. I knew he was still talking about his mother waiting for the bloom of her cactus.

"Then one day, the two little buds changed color." He sighed.

"It was a sure sign of death."

I wanted to ask how it was that he knew that and whether or not he knew that then, but I could tell that we weren't at a place in the conversation for my questions. He had to tell it all at once, without interruptions.

"Then the bright green stems began to drop. Next morning they dried up, died, and fell out. That's when me and my brothers and sister started to get worried. You know, about how Mama would act if the thing didn't work out like she wanted. We started to think this could be something bad for her."

Lathin seemed to move far away again. His voice came and went like he was in another part of his room. I had to listen very closely to make out what he was saying.

"Mama would say, 'That's alright, Orphus,' that's what she called the thing," Lathin said. "Orphus."

I was surprised that a son could remember something so vivid about his mother from such a long time ago.

" 'Orphus saving all his energy for the big bloom. Ain't you, little buddy? Can't be wasting yourself on those little flowers; you spending all your work on this big one here. Just you wait and see,' she'd say to us."

He stopped.

"Now, here's the thing."

He spoke slowly as if he were teaching me something. I felt him close to the wall.

"I ain't never seen Mama hopeful about anything in her life. She came up hard, you know. So, she just did things to get by. She took care of us the best she could, had a little spirit in church, but mostly she was old even when she wasn't."

His voice became flat, distant.

"It was like she put all her dreams into that handful of dirt and flower, all her ideas about herself and her living, all her hope, in that soft closed shell of desert life."

I felt his voice slide farther away.

"Don't much live in the desert, you know," he said. It sounded like he was suddenly changing the subject.

"I learned this 'cause I been in Arizona for three weeks.

I went to show Mary and her mother the Grand Canyon, but we got lost and all we saw was flat land, brown and gray. Miles and miles and nothing but brown and gray. It was depressing, if you ask me."

I watched the movement of the tree outside the window.

"So now that I know how hard it is to try to find something of color in that drab landscape, how much effort it takes for those tight plants to bloom, I understand why it could have happened, how it could have done what it did. But I didn't then. Nobody did then. We were just as crazy about that thing opening as Mama."

I lifted my head to listen more closely, considering Lathin in the desert, his wife and daughter standing near the road, lost and troubled by the landscape.

He sighed, the exhale long and hard and full.

I waited for the story to finish. I wondered what course it would take. And although I'm not sure how I knew it, it sounded like sadness was about to break.

I braced myself.

"The big bud fell too. Not in a day, of course. Took it about three days. Hanging there like some child on the end of a noose."

He took a breath.

"She prayed to that flower, begging it to open, crying for it to let out its color and prove itself to the world. But it just nodded its head and died."

Lathin didn't say anything else for a while.

I don't know why, looking back, relaying it to somebody

who wasn't there, you wouldn't think the story was so sad. It was just a story about a plant, after all, a cactus that didn't bloom.

There were certainly worse stories he could have told me, worse things he could have shared. But somehow then, hearing him tell it, it was sad. It was terribly sad, a lonesome, awful thing. And I remember after he said what he did and then going quiet, I blinked a tear.

"Never even knew what color it was going to be."

The tree limbs rattled and I turned back to face the window.

"My brother Dreyfus and me went out and found the old plant the next week buried in a ditch behind the house. Clay pot and all. We took a knife and slit open the face of that dried-up bloom still clutching to the arm of that cactus, and I swear it was empty inside, just dust, brown-yellow dust, like pieces of sand. Wasn't nothing in that dream but ashes."

I thought he was finished with the story then. And even though I wasn't sure why he told it, I knew it was a story that stayed with him, shaped him, made him like he was. I could tell at the time that even though it was just a story about a plant, it was one of those formative events in his life, one of those moments that changes a person; and I knew if he had told it to one of the doctors at Holly Pines or one of the social workers, they would have asked him what it meant to him.

I decided not to ask. I didn't need to know everything. I had heard enough.

It was quiet for what seemed like a long time. I watched

the tree outside, the only plant living and alive around me that I had seen since I became a patient at Holly Pines Psychiatric Hospital. I noticed how its branches were thrown about in the wind, dancing and loose. It bent and dipped, the perfect partner.

Then finally, Lathin spoke again. He apparently had more to tell about his mother. "We all brought Mama flowers," he said. "Clumps of bluebells and cornflowers, spider plants, baskets of jasmine and lily of the Nile. I even snuck into the white people's gardens and dug up lilac, zinnias, and bushy aster."

"Tasmine, my oldest sister, rolled out layers of wild clover and carpet grass. Dreyfus went looking in the woods for new blooms. We tried anything to get her to pay attention to the sunlight or the change of seasons or the way she had started to let her stockings fall down around her ankles."

I leaned my head against the wall, to be closer to him, I guess.

"I spooned cocoa in her milk and dropped rose petals in her bathwater, but nothing worked. She just turned her face against the plants, let them all die, quit eating sweets, stopped watching the sky, and would not tend to another living thing."

He was quiet for a while and I kept following the pattern of the wind as it blew about the tree and the dust and the path of light.

"Finally, when I was old enough, or when I thought I was old enough, I packed up my stuff and left."

There was a roll of thunder in the distance.

"I decided that I was never going to stand around waiting for something else to fill up a corner with my color. That I was never going down on my knees, begging some flower to bloom because I think I can't, that I ain't never depending on something else to wear its bright red heart on its arm because I don't think I got one of my own."

And then something strange happened. The conversation, the story, it all broke apart. It seemed what he was talking about shifted somehow. I don't know how to explain it, but the memories he shared became like the wind outside. All of a sudden there was a spilling out of nature, a howl, a speeding-up of everything.

I heard sounds coming from his room, odd sounds, movement of a body and furniture. And it sounded like there was pacing, like an animal caught and locked in a cage.

Something slammed against the wall.

He continued to talk. His voice had become raised, sharp. "I did and tried everything I knew to get her back, bring her back. I bought chocolates and tiny china dolls and little dishes of butterscotch ice cream."

I was confused. I no longer knew whom he was talking about.

"I tried taking her to the movies and the soda shop, even out to the park. But she just seemed to close up around herself. She just melted inside like candle wax."

I watched out the window as the tree bent and swayed. The leaves fell off in swirls. The shadows shook like ghosts all around the room. I started to feel a little cold and I pulled the blanket tightly around me.

I tried to follow the line of Lathin's story, his mother's unwillingness to enter into life, but suddenly it seemed as if he were now talking about somebody else. It was as if another story had collided into the first one he was telling, like two cars hitting head-on along some dark highway. I did not understand what he was telling me and I was afraid to stop him and ask.

"Doctors said it was something that happened. That maybe some night when I was gone and she was by herself that something happened, and I didn't know nothing about it."

There was another thump, a crash, but not as loud. I tried to see if it had come from outside the window or from Lathin's room. I wasn't sure.

He went on.

"That maybe she let somebody in the apartment or maybe it was when she walked home from school. But I never let her walk by herself and she knew better than to open her door to a stranger."

He seemed even farther away. His voice, his story, pulling away from the wall, pulling away from me and our conversation.

"And I never was gone more than a couple of hours.

"Never," he growled. "I made sure of that. And I taught her how to be careful. I taught her how to be when she was by herself. I taught her those things."

His voice was loud and I worried that Calvin would soon be at my door or at his door.

Lathin kept going.

"I asked everybody. I talked to everybody. Nobody knew nothing. Nobody!" he yelled.

"And my baby girl wouldn't never say nothing. She just dropped way back behind her eyes, way back behind who she was, and the only thing I could make out was a quiet little way she'd call out the names of flowers right before she went off to sleep."

He sounded desperate, broken. I wanted to comfort him, but I didn't know how. I had become afraid of him.

"It was the only time she'd talk, the only time she'd say anything." His voice was tight, stretched. "I begged her. I pleaded with her. 'Tell me, baby, tell your daddy what happened.' But she wouldn't say nothing. Call out the names of little flowers she'd seen, but that's all she'd tell me. That's all she'd say."

He whispered, "Daisies, black-eyed Susans, bachelor's buttons. Names of plants she learned from her teacher at school. Names I had taught her. Names of the flowers I had given to her grandmother, names that didn't change anything."

The air conditioner churned on and I tried to understand his story, this new story. I tried to put it together with the story of his mother, the story of the cactus.

"She quit me. She wouldn't tell me nothing. She just went away somewhere. Just like her mama, just like her grandma. She just quit."

He stopped for a minute and I began to make the connection of the memory about his mother and the loss of her dream and this new story, this horrible story of something that happened to his little girl.

"The next day I called her aunt to come get her and I burned down that fancy little boutique where the window display looked like a garden of dresses and the apartment where we lived where people were saying that bad things happened to children. I hitched out of town while the yellow flames drank up half the downtown."

The tree slammed against the glass and it startled me and I guess it startled Lathin too. He waited a few minutes before continuing.

"She was little, but she could have said something. She could have told me what it was. She could have trusted me a little bit enough to make it better. But she didn't. She gave up. She didn't even try. Somebody hurt my baby and she wouldn't tell me nothing."

I heard another loud noise, like he had thrown something across his room, a shoe, a book, I wasn't sure.

"All you women with your hollow eyes, your untelling tongues, your lifeless dreams."

I pulled away from the wall, suddenly feeling his anger now moving toward me.

"You and your sorry little folded-up paper wishes, your dance lessons that take you nowhere, your empty windowsills, and your stingy hearts."

I was confused by what was happening on the other side of the wall, by his stories, his anger. I leaned away from him while the tree pounded against the glass.

"Don't make no sense how you can waste your whole life giving up. It's pitiful. You're pitiful."

I was stunned. I didn't know how to respond. Lathin was like a different man, a different person.

He was suddenly so irrational, sliding out of one story about his mother and into another that seemed like it had to do with his daughter, and then he was mixing it all up with me. I didn't know what to say. And the windstorm rattled the things outside.

He was not waiting for a reply. He kept going further and further into this mixing-up of women's lives.

"Sitting around in some rich people's head hospital because you all twisted up in something your mama wanted and couldn't get. You pathetic little white girl, why don't you do something about your life instead of sitting around crying about it?"

I stood up and faced the wall, faced him, unsure of what I was going to do, thinking that perhaps I ought to call for help, that perhaps Lathin was becoming dangerous and that I needed some protection from this man locked up in the room next door.

He didn't let up. Now it was if he had completely turned his wrath on me. He had moved from his mother to his daughter and was now squarely in confrontation with me.

"Why don't you just kill yourself? Save a whole lot of people from worrying with you and your insurance company a lot of money."

And then it became clear, what he was saying, how he had defined me, sized me up. And just like that, in a split second, I hated him, hated the things he was yelling, hated the woman he had decided I was.

I hated that he thought he knew me after a few hours of conversation, that after just telling him a few memories about how I dreamed or what I thought that he knew the kind of person I was, that he knew me in some profound way that nobody else ever had. And suddenly, I don't know why, I don't know how, but I screamed back. Like an animal trapped and provoked, I fought back.

"Oh, and your life is so much better than mine."

I wasn't sure what I was going to say next. I only knew that just as the tree and the wind were no longer partners in a night dance, we were no longer friends sharing our histories.

Now like the two instruments of nature battling outside my window, Lathin Hawkins and I had begun an engagement of war, a struggle against each other.

"Lord knows how much fulfillment I've given up or my mother's given up not burning things down, abandoning a child, and being in prison slitting my wrists!"

He wasn't about to stop with that.

"Yeah, well at least I got to choose my life."

I started to feel stronger in a way, more energy than I had had in a long time. It was exhilarating. I felt the blood pulse faster, my face flush.

"And who got to choose Mary's, huh?" I pushed. "Guess you're real proud of the choice you made for her."

I didn't even care that I was yelling. I was alive in some new way I had never been before. I was set loose and flying.

"You're so smug sitting over there, thinking you're stronger than me because *you* got to *choose* prison! You think you've lived such an exemplary life because you had the guts to try and kill yourself and I didn't! That you went through with it and I checked into a hospital. You think that makes you better?" I kicked at the wall between us.

"I don't have to sit around and wonder what I might have done, what I could have done." His voice was as sharp as a needle.

"No, you get to sit in a cell and think about all the damage you did, how you weren't there when your daughter needed you, and how she grew up without a parent around."

"Don't worry about my daughter! Worry about your own self! You're so wrapped up in your mama's mistakes, you don't even have your own life. All you got is hers!"

"That's not true!" I yelled in reply. "My mama didn't choose my life! I chose my life! Me! I have everything I want."

"Yeah, then why you carry that newspaper clipping around with you? Why you still know it like you wrote it?"

I was wishing I had never told him that story about my mother. I was wishing I had never answered his question about chapel, never engaged myself in this ludicrous conversation.

"Why you sitting in a goddamn library surrounded by the stuff other people dream? Why ain't you living your own life instead of reading about everybody else's?"

I slammed my fists against the wall.

"Least I didn't leave my child! Least I didn't run off

from the person I was supposed to love! Least I didn't quit caring about somebody just because they wouldn't talk to me.

"No, 'cause you ain't got nobody to love!"

His words stung, drew blood, and once I didn't respond, he smelled his victory.

"You don't, do you?"

And I heard the smugness in his voice. I heard the sneer, the way he almost laughed when he realized what he had said and how it shut me up.

"You don't know what the hell you're talking about!" I screamed, but it was too late. The damage had been done and we both knew it. "You don't have the right to talk to me like that! You don't get to say it. Not you! Especially you!"

"Somebody needs to talk to you like that! You need to hear it from somebody!"

I was silenced by his rage, by my rage; and I dragged the chair from the window to the wall and sat down with my back against him. A branch from the tree cracked and dropped on the sidewalk below. There was a loud bang as it fell.

I sat like that for a while, listening to the storm, listening to the scratching of the limbs against the window, the falling pieces of tree, the whirl of the wind all around me, and I sat thinking about what we had said to each other, all the horrible things we had said. And in the fit of the storm and in the lull of our struggle, I realized that I could not remember the last time I had fought with someone, the last time I had felt such anger.

It suddenly seemed to me as if I had lived my entire life being polite, being surrounded by people who were polite. I had been living by the rules in the library, never speaking above a whisper, never addressing how I felt, how I hurt, only giving out information, facts, figures, never engaging in conflict. And in spite of the irrational way the conversation had gone, the way he got all the stories mixed up, the way he had turned on me, made his story about me, I knew he was right.

I knew the things he said about my life were true. I knew because what he said hurt so much. I stared at the wall straight ahead as if the writing had become clear.

In that moment, I understood then what I understand now, that truth has a way of doing that, pinching you so tight that you have to see it, have to turn to it. And you can wail and scream and even wrestle it, but it always comes out exactly as it is.

You can bend it, loosen it, stretch it, but it will never break. And even though it's been said that the truth will set you free, right then it felt like it was suffocating me. I was smothered by what he had said. I could hardly breathe.

Lathin had uncovered a crude, hidden stone. Way beneath the veneer of mild manners, down below the surface of gentility and Southern charm, layered under the façade of a librarian's pleasant helpfulness was a stratum of stony memories that shifted and slipped and now rolled to the edge of my mind.

The prison inmate had managed to do what no one had done before. He had seen and pulled the one dangling thread that hung from the hem of my spirit. He wrapped it hard around his fingers, teased at it first, and then yanked loose the contents that spilled and finally fell out into the open.

The wind pulled the tree down and then back, hard. Then it stopped, and with less energy this time, picked up again. The storm was not over.

Of course, in our struggle, Lathin and I had gotten too loud. The yelling and the things being thrown against the wall between us had caused a commotion. We had stopped being careful and I knew the others had heard us. So, I was not at all surprised when I heard the hall door open and close. I heard the footsteps coming near. I didn't, however, run to my bed as I had earlier. I didn't drop down and pretend to be asleep. I just stayed where I was, in the chair by the wall. I just stayed exactly as I was.

My door opened and the overhead light came on.

"All right, what is going on? What are you yelling about and why aren't you asleep?"

It was Calvin. Since I had already seen him a couple of hours before, I wondered if he was the only person working that shift or if he was always the one who got sent during the night when there was any kind of trouble. Whatever the reason he was in my room, I was glad it was him and not the first attendant I met when I got to Holly Pines, Farrell. In my time at the hospital, I never felt judged by Calvin. I thought we had a mutual respect for each other.

For a few minutes, however, before I answered him, I considered very carefully my response. I thought of telling

Calvin about Lathin, about how he started talking to me
earlier in the evening. I knew that I had lots of options of
what to report to Calvin. I could say that I tried to ignore
the patient next door, but he had harassed me all night
long. I thought I might explain how I had found out that
they had a prison inmate staying next door to me and how
dangerous he was and how much trouble I felt the arrangement had caused me.

I could tell Calvin that I was scared of Lathin, that he
was saying mean and nasty things to me, that I wanted to
talk to the administrator and I was going to sue the hospital
for putting me in such terrible conditions. I could play up
the role of the victim for all that it was worth. I knew it was
a way to go. I knew it could work.

It wouldn't have taken a lot for me to get Lathin into trouble, make them move him to another room or to another
hall, even take him back to the prison where he had come
from. I thought about how I could even say that he was trying to escape and he was hoarding medications. I bet they
could even find some if they searched him. That would give
even more credence to my allegations. There were so many
things I could use against him.

I was sure that in my state of anger and confusion and
facing the mean truth, I could have easily turned on some
tears to show just how upset I was. I was certain that crying
would make my story even more believable. And I knew
that Calvin hated to see anybody cry, that unlike Farrell or
one of the nurses, he was the perfect one for that show.

I knew this about the night attendant because it had

only been a few days earlier that I had heard him explain to a nurse why he was no longer in college, why he had quit working on his degree in social work.

"I just can't stand it when they get all emotional," he replied, referring to the patients at Holly Pines. "I don't like to hear all the gore of people's lives. I'd rather just make their beds or give them a pill."

I was waiting in line to use the phone at the time. I was waiting to call Mama and give her my daily report.

"I can't stand just listening to it. I need to do something. I'm thinking about being a dental assistant."

The nurse had laughed at that, patted him on the back like she was proud of him, and laughed again.

I turned to look out the window, thinking long and hard about what I could do to pay Mr. Lathin Hawkins back for his spiteful words. I thought of how easy it would be to manipulate Calvin and have the whole thing move along as I wanted.

I thought about where he was in his room and I figured he was next door listening very closely to what I was going to say.

I waited.

Calvin waited.

But I knew what was going to happen. I knew what I was and was not going to do. Once I considered all of my options I knew I wasn't going to cry or say anything to get Lathin in trouble. I wasn't going to take advantage of Calvin and I wasn't going to pretend anything was more than what it really was.

I didn't make up a story or feign harassment. I wasn't going to lie to Calvin or to myself. And I was clear that I refrained from making anything up not because I was a good person or because I felt sorry for Lathin.

I didn't make something up to get Lathin in trouble because I knew that I needed him. I knew he was the one who was going to pull me out of the dark hole I had fallen into, and right at that moment, I was glad that I was at least awake enough to recognize it. I stared out the window.

A few seconds went by and I felt Calvin close behind me. He had waited all he could stand. I would have to tell him something. He needed to know what protocol he would have to follow. He had rules. He needed order.

"I had a bad dream so I got up to catch my breath."

I turned around to face him.

I felt him study me. I allowed it.

"You want me to call the nurse to get you something? You want Ambien or a Xanax?"

"No, I'm fine now." I lifted my face so he could see my eyes. I knew that he would want to see them. I knew mine were clear and steady. There were no tears. There was no distress. I was speaking a truth in a way that the attendant wanted to hear it.

And then I got up from the chair, leaving it by the wall, and Calvin watched as I pulled the covers off the floor and placed them on the bed and lay down. He glanced around the room carefully, nodded at me, switched off the light, and shut the door. I heard him check the lock and then walk to the next room.

I saw his flashlight come on as he peered in at Lathin through the window. He didn't go in. It was very quiet. Then Calvin turned off the flashlight, walked up the hall, and was gone.

Several minutes passed. I looked at my watch. It was now four thirty in the morning; and there was still a lot more that had to be said. The wind had slowed, then died down, and the tree stood full and alone outside the window.

It was silent in our rooms for a very long time.

SEVEN

551.2

ℰARTHQUAKES

"You still against the wall or did you get in bed?"

He didn't reply.

I decided finally to change my clothes and get into my pajamas. I had not bothered to get out of what I was wearing once we started talking, and even though it was almost morning, almost time to dress into the clothes for the next day, I thought it might feel better to get more comfortable at least for a couple of hours.

I went over to the closet and opened the drawer at the bottom. I took off my T-shirt and folded it, placing it on the top shelf. Then I pulled off my jeans and straightened them, smoothing them down while I hung them on the hanger. I took off my socks and threw them in my bag of dirty clothes.

I put on one of the two pairs of pajamas I had brought

with me to the hospital, a yellow silk pair with thin white stripes. I switched every couple of nights, changing from the new ones, the yellow ones, with an old pair of green ones that Mama got me a few years earlier. I bought the yellow ones, the silk pair, when I knew I would be a hospital inpatient, when I realized that the group therapy and the paper bag imaging weren't going to work. I thought they would cheer me up. I smiled thinking of that.

I put on a clean pair of socks because my feet were cold. I shut the closet door and walked over to the bed. I crawled in and just started talking. I wasn't even sure if Lathin was listening anymore. I wasn't sure if he was in bed asleep or was still sitting by the wall. I didn't know anything about what he was doing. I could hear nothing from next door.

"Up until the time I was a teenager my mother used to leave me at my grandmother's every summer."

I positioned myself so that I curled like a baby, facing away from the wall. I guess at that point, even though I knew he was the one who had unlocked a small hidden door in my heart, it didn't really matter if he was listening. I had reached the point where I was going to say what needed to be said.

"She did it so that she wouldn't have to worry about me while she was at work," I explained. "We always lived in apartment buildings or trailer parks and 'everybody knew too much of everybody else's business,' she used to say."

I paused and considered Lathin and his story about Mary,

a child alone in an apartment. I thought about the things he said, the fears a father has for his daughter and I realized maybe my mama had been right.

"Besides, she thought being out in the country with my cousins would be good for me, help me get some social skills, teach me how to relate to children my own age since I was always a little uppity. You know, one of those kids more comfortable with adults than with other children?"

I waited for some response, something to let me know that he was listening, that we were still in conversation, but there was nothing.

"Mama was worried I'd grow up and never have any friends. She knew the moving around was hard on me and I guess she thought that if I had at least some stability in the summers, I'd be a better person, thereby making her a better mother."

I folded my arms around me under the blanket. I knew Mama always worried about how she fared as a mother, that she was always measuring herself against other women with children.

"Grandma lived in Emit, North Carolina. It's near Zebulon, in Johnston County. You heard of it?"

Lathin still didn't say anything, and I realized that now I was the one talking without a response, that the roles were reversed from earlier in the evening and I was just as he had been in the beginning of the conversation. I was asking for something I wasn't sure I'd get. Of course, by then it didn't matter. I had a lot I needed to tell. I had a lot to say and even if no one was listening, it was going to be said.

And so, the story began.

It's *TIME* SPELLED backwards," I said out loud, remembering how PeeDee figured that out when we were in the third grade. "*Emit* is *time* spelled backwards," I said, this time just to myself, just to remember how it sounded to hear PeeDee's words.

"Emit and Johnston County, North Carolina, is all tobacco and cotton fields, Angus beef cattle, laying hens, hogs, usually a hybrid breed, and an occasional goat and mule. I've heard that there's a few ostrich ranches and daylily farms now but there wasn't any of that when I was growing up. Most everybody made their living on the cancer weed.

"Just your basic pork, beef, and cigarette industry. Farmers aren't known for their creative choices, you know. It's just about survival for those folks. What can I grow and pay my bills? That's what they used to say.

"Granddaddy was a farmer. He was like everybody else. Cotton, soybeans, tobacco; he rotated. And he always had a lot of animals out to pasture somewhere. Everybody that knew him said he was rich because he was able to buy up a lot of land during the Depression. I don't know, since my grandma always seemed as poor as a church mouse to me, and I never saw any farm money. Neither did Mama, as far as I know.

"Mama hated Granddaddy. Oh, she cried when he passed, like things had gotten patched up between them, but she didn't mean it. She told me all this much later because he died not long after I was born. And she said it was a good thing that I didn't know him because a person didn't need any extra people to hate."

I stopped and wondered what she might have meant and whether or not I had anyone at that time in my life that I hated. I don't think I've really hated anybody, except maybe myself. But that's not the same, I don't think.

"She never told me what happened between them. She always went silent when I asked her about him. She seemed to close up as soon as I posed the question. It was like she took some vow or made some promise to herself that she wouldn't even speak his name. I don't know what it was.

"I always just imagined that he was hard and mean and that when the doctor came out of my grandmother's bedroom to tell her husband that his firstborn was a little pink girl and not the boy he was planning for, not the worker to help him on the farm, or the one to take him out of debt, that he just hated her from the start. I don't know about any of this, of course, I just had to make this up for myself."

I thought about how Mama's face would go stonelike when she talked about him, how she seemed to have all the bricks in place, building that wall around her emotions, making sure she wouldn't have to say anything that opened her.

"I figure Mama thought I'd do better on the farm than she did. That maybe since Granddaddy wasn't there to snatch the chicken feed out of my hand because I wasn't spreading it across a wide-enough circumference or yank the reins from me because I was not holding them firmly or slap me across the face like I figure that he did her just because she was in his way, that maybe I could grow an appreciation for the land and for working it that she never got. I mean I guess that's why she sent me there. She, of course, never really said.

"The first time she drove me down there we stopped at the turnoff to their house. I turned to look at her and she just stopped driving to wait for what I was going to say. 'You mad at me?' I asked her. We were almost at Grandma's driveway, almost close to where her family could see us drive in. And she put the car in park and held my face in her hands, soft and easy, like what she was going to say was important, necessary.

" 'Baby, no. I could never be mad at you.' And she pulled me into her, squeezing me next to her. 'I just think you'll like it here, that you'll have a little fun without me.'

"We sat in that car all wrapped up in each other, small and unsure, hard to see where she started and I ended.

"Turns out she was right. I really enjoyed my summers on the farm. I really liked being away from town. I think in the beginning I was always more of a country girl than she was."

From that very first visit, I always unfolded at Grandma's. I breathed more deeply, slept better, felt more easy with myself and the world. There were so many things I loved about being on a farm.

"I stayed with Grandma at night, but all day I was with PeeDee and Elva and Maxine. They're my cousins. They're Aunt LuEller's daughters. LuEller's my mother's sister, the youngest. She was, I'm pretty sure, the favored child, the one who grew up sure of herself, sure of her life.

"She was the one my granddaddy loved. For some reason, he was ready for a daughter when LuEller was born. It doesn't make any sense to me, but everybody says it's so, even Grandma and LuEller, so it must have been true.

"When Granddaddy died, he left half of the farm to Grandma and the other half to LuEller. Mama was living in Raleigh at the time, not too far away. She went home to hear the settling of the estate, to be there when it was all said and done. But after the reading of the will, she took off from Johnston County and came back to Raleigh ready to move again. It was as if she was trying to get even farther away from her father even though he was dead.

"I guess even his memories were too mean. I always wondered if such a thing was possible. Mama never said what she thought, but I could always tell when she had her daddy on her mind. She bore a look that never showed itself except when she was thinking about him. It was tight and frozen, like something dead a long time.

"LuEller stayed in Emit. She had already built a house right beside Granddaddy, already married a man that everybody says is the spitting image of Cranford Scope Hackett. That's my granddaddy's whole name.

"LuEller married Jacob Lowery and he farmed with Granddaddy until the crops lost money and he had to take a public job to supplement what he took in from the land. He was never mean to me, pleasant and nice in that kind of distant-relative way. I think he was good to his girls when they were growing up. I never heard any of them complain."

"He installs air-conditioning units, mostly in Smithfield and Wilson. Still farms though. Tomatoes and strawberries mostly. Can't make any money in tobacco anymore. He was always saying that the tobacco farmer was the most screwed man in America, but I never talked to him about that kind of thing. I only heard that when he was talking to some other adults who stopped by to visit.

"Aunt LuEller fixes hair in a little shop Jacob added on to the garage. 'The Curl Up and Dye Shop,' she calls it. Funny, isn't it? The big white sign painted with red and blue letters marked the place from the road. She said it came from a trip she took one time, but I don't know exactly how she came up with the idea.

"I liked my cousins just fine. I was closer to PeeDee than Elva and Maxine. PeeDee was the same age as me, just five months older. She told me that she was named for a state park in South Carolina. Mama and I were going to go there once, but we didn't get that far south. Aunt LuEller used to say PeeDee came out looking like the outdoors, all unbridled and free, so they named her after the best outdoor place they knew, the place where they had met and fallen in love.

"Elva was three years older than us and Maxine was three years younger. And somehow, that three years makes a big difference when it comes to enjoying one another's company in the summer. PeeDee and I had lots of fights with both her older and younger sister. We were always getting into trouble for the way we made fun of Elva and her training bras, how we tormented little Maxine.

"PeeDee and I used to roll up each other's hair, mess around in Aunt LuEller's shop a lot. We played from early in the morning until after supper, everything from kick the can with all the kids who lived around there, to hopscotch, to paper dolls to beauty parlor.

"We'd fish sometimes and ride the tractor with Uncle Jacob, even try to act like we could trap coon and squirrels like her older brother, Lincoln. It was all real outdoor country fun, and PeeDee and I got to be real close.

"Grandma was real nice to me too. She never bothered me at all. Never asked me stuff about Mama's business or stayed after me because I was too messy or too curious. She let me do about anything I wanted and I loved the way she felt when she hugged me.

"Mama said she was never mad at Grandma for how things were between her and her daddy, that Grandma had always tried to work things out, but that even she couldn't fix something that broken. But like I said, I don't know about any of that though since she wouldn't ever talk about how Granddaddy treated her. I did know that Grandma was burdened about what happened between her husband and her daughter, but I also know that it was never something that was discussed. I just heard her when she prayed.

"Grandma and LuEller and all the children went to church a lot. They're Pentecostals, but they would go to anybody's revival. We'd all go to Sunday school on Sunday mornings and Vacation Bible School one week out of the summer. Grandma and LuEller were real serious about churchgoing. They wanted all of us there together.

"Back at home, Mama didn't make me go to church, since she didn't go. She said that she had never felt welcomed in church and that she didn't like the way they were always taking up money. So, except for a few times to that church in Rose Hill, the only time I went was when I was down at Grandma's.

"Every summer we learned all the books, Old and New Testament, and we won prizes for coming every day for Bible School. I didn't love it like PeeDee and Maxine, but it wasn't too bad. The church was always hot and crowded with sticky children. The windows were open and the sounds of tractors were always in the background. The preacher wore black heavy suits and his hair was always slicked back, greasy with some kind of oil or gel. He rolled his eyes back in his head when he prayed and the choir would always hum when he went on too long. We made macaroni pictures and sand art posters in crafts in the children's classes.

"There was one Sunday when Maxine stood up front to recite the Pledge of Allegiance to the Bible. She got so nervous, she peed on herself and the teacher had to walk her home because she was so upset. We laughed for hours about that. Poor Maxine wouldn't leave her room all day.

"The church smelled like hyacinths and old ladies' perfume and Aunt LuEller would twist the top of our ears if we were misbehaving. Grandma plaited up her hair in a wide bun and always dusted her chest with powder before she put on her best dress. She prayed prayers for grace and mercy to come down on her children and her grandchildren and Reverend Hurdy preached long, dry sermons on sin. We sang songs about the blood of Jesus and the broken way we live. And there were always calls to the altar.

"One Sunday when the preacher had preached on keeping the spirit of Easter, I asked PeeDee if she really believed that Jesus rose from the dead. 'I don't know about all that,' she said, braiding her hair in two long pigtails, 'but it does get us out of school a day and me a new pair of black patent leather shoes with the T-strap across the top, so I ain't got no problem celebrating like he did find a way out.

"PeeDee was funny about church. She would cry and act like she was getting saved or convicted or something was happening to her soul and she'd run up to the front near the preacher and fall down, pray real loud and all, then later in the afternoon when we'd be sitting in the barn, she'd say that it was all a joke, that she had done it just for laughs. And I remember that even though she was my favorite cousin, my best friend even, I was not very comfortable with that part of her. She was real two-sided like that."

Just then I thought of PeeDee, not the way I saw her at the last with her arms folded across her chest like she would hold them when we played Dare and then afterward turn her face away from me, lock her knees, close her eyes, and fall back into my arms.

I didn't think of that image, that gray, frozen image, I thought of her when she had talked about church, three days earlier, sitting against a bale of hay, her wild black hair tied back with pieces of tobacco twine, her face red and flushed from the race and the climb up to the top, her fingers locked behind her head, her long and usual sigh of contentment with herself and the day and the appearance of things to come.

"She was a funny girl." I stopped and then added, "And she was the only one to talk to me about my daddy.

"The summer before we turned twelve she had found out about him, found out his name and where he lived and how long Mama dated him before she got pregnant with me. I still don't know how she got all the information that she did. Nobody in the family liked to talk about Mama getting pregnant and not being married, especially Mama. So, I didn't ask much it.

"But that year PeeDee had done a really good job of researching the whole sorry story. She waited to tell me on my birthday. She waited until after the celebration at Grandma's and after I was quite satisfied with everything I had gotten. And then, after the party, PeeDee said that she had a special surprise for me. The truth is, I have never liked surprises, but I guess she didn't know or didn't care. She did it anyway.

"She blindfolded me and walked me out to the barn where we always played, then stood me in front of this table, and took off the scarf from around my eyes. I closed my eyes like she told me to, waiting for the surprise she was giving me. I was actually hoping that it was a puppy or a kitten. I was looking forward to some company. And then, when she said it was okay to do so, I opened my eyes.

"And that was when she showed me a picture of him that I don't to this day know how she got it and a piece of fancy stationery paper on which she had written down his address and even where he worked. She had put a purple candle on the table and a vase of little cottage roses. She was so proud of all that she had done. She figured it was the best present I would ever get.

"Even though I had talked about being curious about who he was and even though we had guessed a lot of times whom it could be, lying in bed imagining how he looked or the size of his hands, somehow having the truth put out there in front of me, written down on a fancy piece of paper and having a picture to go with it, I don't know, it just didn't feel as good as I thought it would. Once I knew who he was, saw his name and where he lived, once it was clear that she knew and probably lots of other people knew too, it just sort of made me feel sick to my stomach somehow. Embarrassed or something.

"And then, when it was obvious that I wasn't pleased with her gift, with her surprise, she acted all different, all hurt or something. It was more than disappointment; it was anger, like she was mad that I didn't want her present. She blew out the candle, swept the paper and photograph off the table, and walked away, leaving me alone with the information, with him.

"I hadn't wanted to be rude to her. I just wasn't ready for what she had found out and what she wanted me to know. After all, I had decided to believe that my daddy was dead. I had even made up where he was buried and even bought flowers a few times to pretend I was putting them next to a headstone. And then all of a sudden, it was as if PeeDee brought him up from the grave, like the preacher did Jesus on Easter. It just stunned me is all.

"I know she thought I should like what she gave me, and I did end up keeping the papers. I still have the picture of him. The pretty stationery with his address and place of employment too. But I never called him or anything. I think I just liked it better when he was dead.

"Other than that, other than the surprise from PeeDee in the barn, the feelings about my father and about disappointing her, it was a really nice birthday. Grandma made a chocolate cake with real fudge icing. I had three pieces and a whole bowl of ice cream. I think it was the most I ever ate at a party. Aunt LuEller and Elva put up decorations in the kitchen, cut out HAPPY BIRTHDAY letters and twisted blue and orange crepe paper, and hung them all across the room.

"There were fat, white balloons tied to the tops of all the chairs and cherry lemonade in the crystal pitcher Grandma only used for special occasions. And I got some great presents. Everybody celebrated. Mama had even arrived, bringing me a Kodak camera with snap-on flashbulbs and a diary that had a real lock and key. Uncle Jacob brought out the dollhouse he made complete with a garage and an upstairs. Grandma gave me a short set she had made and a Monopoly game, and I got a real oyster shell necklace from Aunt LuEller and the girls.

"The whole event had been a big lovely surprise since most of my birthdays were flat and lonesome. I never knew anyone to share a personalized pizza party or invite over for a sleepover. It was usually just me and Mama going out to a movie or having a little party at the Waffle House with the other waitresses. Birthdays had never been a big event for the two of us, so when Grandma and Aunt LuEller decided to have my birthday celebration in the summer a couple of months after the real date, when everyone was home, it was quite spectacular. So when I went from having my best birthday I had ever had to going out to the barn where PeeDee added her extra surprise, this big announcement about my father, I just found that it was just about more than I could take, more than I could hold together or find a way to order.

"After that birthday I never celebrated it with family again. I was satisfied with a store-bought cake and going to the movies with Mama. We never had another big summer event in honor of my birth again. It was, in fact, the last time that we all got together for something other than a funeral. I don't know. Maybe things might have been different if we could have managed another birthday celebration together or if that one could have turned out better.

"After that, life changed. Everything changed. There would never be another birthday like that one. There would never be another summer, another season, that felt as full and special. That's the last good thought of Johnston County that I have. Of course, I didn't know any of that at the time. I was just a kid looking for fun.

"The following spring we wrote each other every day. We had big ideas for our next summer. PeeDee got over being mad that I didn't like her present and we were planning for the next season to be the best summer ever. We were going to a church camp for young people, the first time for both of us and we were very excited. It was in the mountains and we were going to learn to canoe and build campfires. There would be lots of other kids from across the state and neither of her sisters was going."

I was so happy to think of a week outdoors, a week alone with my favorite cousin. I was so happy to think about what life was going to bring me.

"Then later, probably sometime in June, Aunt LuEller was going to drive us up to Virginia to pick blueberries and peaches. And she and Uncle Jacob were planning to take everyone to the beach over the Fourth of July. Even Mama was going to join us."

There was even a plan that PeeDee had to find and visit my father, a plan I had not agreed to, but did not say.

"Grandma had promised to teach us how to tat lace and PeeDee was even sure that we would both have boyfriends because a Boy Scout camp had opened on the farm next to theirs and she said there were always boys camping out and swimming in the Timmons Lake."

I kept all of PeeDee's letters that spring, read them over and over, every night.

"I was packed for at least a month before I left. I pestered Mama to death making sure that she had asked off work the very first day school was out so that she could drive me down the earliest chance I had. I wanted that summer of my thirteenth year to last as long as it could. It's true, I now know, what people say, that you should be careful what you ask for.

"PeeDee moved in at Grandma's with me. When I got there, she had already put her stuff in the closet and filled up three of the drawers. We had decided the summer before that the next year that she should just come over and stay with me. And since she was tired of having to share her room with Elva anyway, she was glad to get out and join me. Grandma didn't mind at all.

"We pulled the two twin beds together and borrowed sheets for a double bed and took down all of Grandma's knickknacks. We decorated the room like we wanted by filling the shelves with bird nests and stones that we found. And we painted pictures and stuck them in the frames she had on the wall. We settled right in. We'd talk until real early in the morning, long conversations, deep conversations about secrets and hopes, all the stuff we didn't say to anybody else.

"And then we'd sleep late and spend all day playing. For the first three weeks it was everything I thought it would be, only better. We helped Grandma put up peach preserves and make blueberry jam. She bought us yards of thread and we started learning how to tat. It was the most domestic I've ever been."

That summer especially, Grandma's house was thick with the sugary smells. There was a draw from the window fans day and night and there were always a carefully tended garden and flower beds.

I loved the way I felt when I was in her house. It was the

only time in my life I ever felt at home, ever felt as if I truly belonged to a place, a shelter, a family.

"We did a lot of stuff outside too. I know I don't look like much of any outdoorsy kind of person, but in those days I was more, I don't know, strong and tomboyish. I wasn't too worried about getting dirty or getting hurt. I liked to be outside, liked to play more then.

"Not like PeeDee, of course. She was always more adventuresome than me. She swam like a fish, climbed trees faster than any of the boys around the county, and she wasn't afraid of anything. She picked up frogs and lizards. And she was forever chasing snakes. She was crazy like that. More so than me.

"She was the one who taught me how to hold a catfish so I wouldn't lose him or get cut by his fin. And even though Mama says it was she who showed me, it was PeeDee who took me to the thicket of honeysuckle vines at the edge of the woods where you could squeeze underneath them and feel like you were tangled in honey. It was the sweetest feeling you could ever have and it was always how I think Heaven will smell.

"One morning not long after, we had gone to Virginia to pick fruit, June 24th."

The date is forever clear in my mind, even when it isn't said. Even when no one else knows. That date. That day is like a day of death. It is never forgotten for those who somehow die.

"We were walking along the creek looking for arrowheads. Sometimes you could find them at the edge or caught along the sides of bigger rocks. There were always a lot of them near Grandma's house. I never really knew why.

"PeeDee said there was a man in Selma, a little town up the road from where they lived, who was buying them and that we could make a lot of money if we collected a bunch. She had a lot of ways that we could make money. Anyway, I already had three in my pocket and she was sticking the ones she found in her shoes that she had slung across her shoulders."

I didn't take mine, but rather left my pair on the bank. Not long after I left them, I had wished I brought them with me. I could see that she tied hers together and used them like a bag. Like so many of the things PeeDee did, it just made good sense.

"It was just after breakfast and the sun wasn't very hot. In fact, where we were, in the widest part of the stream, the trees made a canopy over our heads and the water was really cold."

Once we started walking there was a chill along my ankles and my fingers turned dark red. I wanted to dry off and wait to go back when it was warmer, but PeeDee had already made up her mind about the morning activity. She wasn't about to stop.

"We were talking about what we would do with the money. I said that we should combine what we got as soon as we got it and buy a big plastic float to take to the beach. But she had a better idea.

"She thought we should save all the money until the end

of the summer, add it to other money we could make turning in glass bottles to the grocery store and mowing the grass, and have her mom take us to the amusement park in Charlotte for a big end-of-summer fun day. It was a nice plan, and I agreed that it was much better than the plastic beach float.

"PeeDee stopped and heard the noises first, before I did. I was still bending down, sifting through the fool's gold and pieces of flint, talking about the camp in July and whether or not I should have Mama send me another swimsuit since the one I had brought with me was two pieces and sometimes came untied up top.

"I saw her after she had already crawled up the bank and was running toward the bend in the creek where a sweetgum tree grew out from the side and made a nice place to look out over the meadow and the deepest part of the stream. She was up the tree calling me before I was even out of the water. I still don't know how she got up there so fast. I mean I stood up and she was completely gone from where she had just been.

"Of course I followed her. I always followed PeeDee. That's how we did things, how we worked, how our relationship made sense and gave us what we wanted.

"I saw her shoes thrown down under the tree and I started climbing. I didn't go as high because she always went up to where the limbs were small and the trunk was much too narrow for me. I went just as far as I needed to be so that I could see what she had been yelling about."

She was standing six or seven feet above my head and the branch she was on was no thicker than my arm. She waved and jumped, hollering to be seen.

"It was a stupid Boy Scout troop, putting up their tents. They were camping in the pasture next to the creek. There was about ten or fifteen of them, young boys really. They weren't anybody we would have been interested in somewhere else.

"It was nothing, and I even felt a little mad at her for making me run through the water and up the bank and then climb that old tree just to see a bunch of boys. It was stupid and I didn't want to be up that tree. I didn't want to cause any scene for those dumb boys. They weren't even our age. I don't know why she wanted to mess with them.

"When the limb broke, I first thought it was mine. So I turned and faced the trunk to hold on. I squeezed my eyes shut because I thought I was on my way down. I kept thinking that I probably wouldn't die since I wasn't so very high, but that I would definitely get hurt so I braced myself to fall, holding on to the dark face of that tree. I could smell the damp wood. I was waiting to drop and break a leg or cut myself on the sharp tiny branches below me.

"But it turns out it wasn't my branch. It wasn't me that was falling. I was still grasping the trunk, still safe, still secure. It was PeeDee. In all of her jumping and screaming, she slipped and fell from her place. In an instant she just shifted and dropped. It was awful. The noises, all the pieces breaking.

"She just fell and fell. It was like something happening in slow motion. Every noise, every limb cracking, it was slow and loud as thunder.

"She grabbed at anything, at bark, at leaves, at the branches that were falling with her, she even brushed against my back, but I couldn't turn around to catch her because I was afraid of falling too. I couldn't turn around and stop her or hold her because I knew I would just land on top of her.

"The whole way down she never cried or screamed or said anything. All I heard was the sound of the snapping of limbs, the hollow stirring of leaves, and my own heart pounding. It was loud and terrible. And when the sounds stopped, she finally landed, facedown in the creek. It was a silence like I had never heard, an emptiness, like the very breath in every living thing around us blew out at once. As if we all died at once and together.

"It wasn't the fall that killed her," I said quietly.

"They say she actually died from drowning. They say that she might have survived the fall if she hadn't taken water into her lungs."

The words fell like stones from my lips and they kept coming. There was nothing to stop them now.

"And even though no one ever said it out loud to me, I know Aunt LuEller and Uncle Jacob thought it, whispered it to each other late in the night, that Grandma and Elva and Lincoln and Maxine looked at me differently from then on. That even that stupid Boy Scout troop, all of them dressed in their smart tan uniforms, moving together toward us like a flock of brown ducks rising from water, even they thought I should have done something. I could see right away that they thought it was my fault that the girl in the sweetgum tree that had been calling to them, the girl waving from the top, so freely like a tiny bird, was dead because of me."

I saw them coming at me, first curious, and then concerned, and then suddenly turning into judge and jury, casting blame in my direction. They arrived at the tree all ordered and in time, at first looking at me with worry and fear, and then, once they saw PeeDee lying like she was, their manners just changed. Everything about how they spoke to me, the way they looked at me changed. And it became all so easy, the way that I immediately dropped into the guilt and was lost forever.

"If I had gotten down right away, if I had been willing to let go of that tree trunk and jump beside PeeDee, if I had just rolled her on her back, if I had just been willing to let go and climb down, like she would have done for me, like anybody would've done, then everything would be different. Everybody would be different. I would be different."

I stopped talking and suddenly realized that I will always remember the smell of that tree and the way the black trunk felt inside my arms, false and stiff. I will never be able to forget how my fingernails dug in the bark, the small dark flecks still there when the man with the Boy Scouts, the leader, talked me down, caught me by the waist, and turned me around so that he filled the empty place where the trunk had just been.

As long as I live, I will never forget the way those Boy Scouts stared at me, the way their eyes looked me up and down but wouldn't meet mine, the way they glanced away like I was too pathetic even to see. As long as I live, I will forever remember the cut of their eyes and how they were standing too close, their shirts and shorts stiff from ironing, blue and red handkerchiefs tied in knots around their necks, the clean and sharp manner in which they turned aside so as not to look at me too long.

Those stupid boys watched until I saw them and then spun their heads around in some quick way to stare at the sky or the water or the man who was giving them instructions to go back to the meadow and find the other leader. And I will never forget how they turned to one another or the tree or the lifeless body of PeeDee, but would not look me in the eyes.

Or how will I forget Aunt LuEller's blank face when the man walked in the shop behind me, carrying PeeDee like she was a doll, her back limp and broken, stretched across his arms, her long black hair wet and dripping with pieces of leaves and twigs and small clumps of moss, her mouth pulled open like she was wanting to speak? How can I forget the way Aunt LuEller yanked PeeDee away from him, like it was something he had done to cause her to look like that? I will always remember the way she screamed and fell on her knees still cradling PeeDee, calling for her to wake up, to get up, to stop playing this ugly game. The way she finally glanced up at me like I was the one who was supposed to be dead, like I was the one who was always supposed to be dead.

There was a woman in the salon chair who jumped up and ran to the phone after we walked in. I can still see her hair wrapped in pieces of aluminum foil, a big silver plastic sheet draped around her neck. I can still remember how she looked like a science project, a lesson about electricity with wires standing straight out from her head.

And I know that the smell of permanent solution and creek water and the sweetgum bark, how it all blended together will represent forever for me the stale, lingering stench of death.

I can never forget Grandma's arms and how she picked me up and carried me all the way to her house. How I was too big for her and my feet dragged down along the ground behind us. How she pulled off my clothes and sat me in the bathtub and poured steaming hot water on me, trying to wash away the stains and the smell and the thoughts of something so horrible, something so awful that I would never be the same again.

How she knelt down next to me, getting the sleeves of her housedress wet, how she called me sunny girl, rubbed witch hazel lotion on my back, and put me in the bed. How all this was done before she had heard that I could have saved PeeDee.

I cleared my throat and went on. "Mama drove in late that night. She slipped in the bed beside me while she thought I was sleeping. I felt her next to me, her uselessness, her pity and self-hatred for sending me there, letting me go to that place where she almost died inside. And I knew as she lay beside me, all broken up and splintered, that I should turn over and let her know that I was all right, that she was all right, that we would be all right. But I didn't. I didn't do a thing. I didn't turn over. I didn't cry. I didn't say a word or hug her back. All I could do was lie there, pressed around myself and my weak, weak heart. And with that, that not turning around and facing what needed to be faced, not doing what needed to be done for a second time, my life was made. I became what I am."

The tree outside suddenly snapped in a short early morning wind and I was immediately jolted back to where I was, who I was with. I stopped what I was saying, stopped the way the memories had taken hold of me, and got up from the bed with the blanket and pillow and walked over to the wall. I sat down and leaned against it.

I had not heard a sound from next door and I didn't even know if Lathin had been listening to my sorry story. I didn't know what he thought or what he would say. I didn't even know if he had been able to hear me, how loud I had really talked. And yet, somehow I knew that it didn't matter anymore. None of it, our story, our dialogue, our little lies, none of it mattered. I had been talking for almost an hour and it didn't matter one bit that the only one who had heard it was me.

"So, you see, you're right," I said, taking us back to what we had said together, back to his words about me, his ugly truth, what he had broken open inside me.

"I am pitiful. I am wedged into my mother's dream, crammed into something she wanted and couldn't have, some daughter I would never be, wrapped up in mistakes."

I dropped my head to my chest, pulling my knees up and myself around me. "Only, see here's where you're wrong because they weren't her errors, it wasn't her fault. It wasn't my mother who did this to me or made my mistakes. It was mine. My mistake. My weakness. My fault. And the truth is that you are better than me. You are a better person, made the better choice."

It was quiet in our two rooms, but I was not completely finished. There was one more thing to say to him.

"You may have left Mary, but at least you didn't kill her. At least you could turn away from yourself and try to stop her from falling. At least you know you tried. You may have lost her, but at least you have that. At least you did something."

I leaned back and with that I didn't expect to hear anything else. I thought it was all done and said. I closed my eyes and just wanted everything to be finished, like the story. I wanted it all to be done, the sorrow, the sadness, the guilt, the living of such a ragged life. I just wanted it to be done.

It was silent for what seemed like a very long time.

And then he spoke. His voice, so near this time, full and smooth. His words, so simple and tender. It was not at all like it had been before, when we argued. It was different. He was different.

"I was a man. A father. Her father."

I didn't move. I just sat listening, spent from all I had shared.

"You were a child," he added. "You were scared. How you think you could have made any other kind of choice?"

I felt him next to me. I heard the calm way he was trying to smooth out the memories, the attempt he was making to put right all that I had done wrong.

"A teacher told me once that you are who you're going to be by the time you're twelve. That your personality is already formed." I hesitated. "Do you believe that?"

"I don't know."

"I was thirteen."

I thought about the teacher who had told me this. The easy way she had said it, like it was as harmless as telling the time or giving directions to the cafeteria, how it felt to hear such a thing, to accept such a thing about myself.

"I was already who I am now. I could have been the kind of person who would have reached out and caught her while she fell. I could have been the kind of person who would have jumped right after her and pulled her out of the water. I could have told her to come down before she fell. But I didn't do it then and I wouldn't do it now."

I stopped and then continued.

"Don't you see? It's exactly like you said. I am afraid. I'm too scared to make a choice that might change things so I just make a choice not to do anything. I chose not to do anything and somebody died. PeeDee died."

He waited, like maybe he was thinking about what he wanted to say, like maybe I was right, and then he responded.

"Your little friend made a choice too. Don't forget that. She's the one who climbed too high. That was her doing. Somebody living reckless like that going to fall out of trees or land up dead. I know; I seen people like that all my life."

His voice was so close it seemed as if I could feel his breath.

"She made her choice too. You can't blame yourself for what she did."

Then I snapped myself around, to face him behind the wall.

"What about Mary?"

"What about her?"

"You think that about her?"

"That's not the same," he said.

"How is that?" I asked. "How is it not the same?"

"She didn't have no choice. She didn't have no mama to help her. I left her alone when I should have been with her. She didn't climb up no tree. Somebody hurt her. Somebody did something bad to her. This ain't the same thing. We're talking about you."

"Yeah, but why isn't it the same? You blame yourself just like I do."

I felt his uneasiness, his unwillingness to agree, his hesitation to look at things my way, but it all made sense to me.

"We're just alike, me and you," I said.

I stopped a minute.

"I blame myself for my cousin's death and you blame yourself for Mary's silence. I blame myself for my choice not to help her, not to do anything, and you blame yourself for your choice to be away the time something happened to your daughter." And then I added, "Everybody had a choice of some kind, didn't they?"

"Mary didn't have no choice about what happened to her."

"No, but you were right a while ago, she had a choice whether to die inside or not."

"I don't know what you're talking about now. I was mad back then, talking crazy. How somebody got a choice about how to act when they only nine years old? I was just being foolish."

He took a deep breath like he was still thinking.

"I don't believe she got no choice about what she did. Evil struck her down. She didn't have nothing to do but just go dumb in the face of it."

I replied to him quickly. "Well, I don't think a thirteen-year-old girl should die just because she chooses to climb up a tree too high."

I was quiet for a minute.

Then I spoke again.

"And I don't blame your mama for folding up on herself because something she hoped for couldn't come to pass. And I don't judge my mama for holding back from accomplishing her dream. Sometimes life's just stronger than what we got on the inside. Sometimes evil's just bigger than we are."

And then I stopped talking, and finally, after all that we had said to each other, all the loose talk and the biting accusations, the clenched-jaw revelations and the uncensored disclosures, it grew silent in rooms sixteen and eighteen, the end of the dark north-side hall at Holly Pines.

The wall seemed to melt between us and I leaned against him.

"So tell me your bad dream."

I winced.

"Or don't," he said. "I ain't got to hear that, some things shouldn't be said out loud anyways."

I thought about Lathin, the night, how far we'd come. And I realized after telling the real story, the dream was only a reflection of what had already been told. I doubted that it could really hurt me any worse than the memories had.

"Well, it's not very far off from the story. And it never changes any," I said softly so that only he would hear.

"After more than twenty years, it's always the same."

I took another deep breath.

"I'm playing a game in the woods, with PeeDee, I suppose; I never really see her face."

I leaned back and closed my eyes; the blanket was wrapped tight around me.

"I can hear her though, calling me, like from that swimming pool game, Marco Polo."

I stopped to explain the game to him in case he didn't know it.

"One person has their eyes closed and calls out 'Marco,' and everyone else has to yell out 'Polo,' and the one with their eyes closed tries to find and tag someone else."

I waited to see if he was going to say he understood, but he just listened.

"We played it a lot growing up. Kids dive in and swim to the other side of the pool, trying to fool the one who is supposed to be blind. The only rule is that when the person says, 'Marco,' you've got to stop where you are, no diving then, no swimming away, and you've got to say 'Polo.' It's the only way to make it fair."

I reached over and picked up the pillow from beside me and placed it behind my back.

"Only in my dream, we aren't in a pool, there isn't any water, except the rain. And it's not a heavy one, not a downpour; it's just misting. It's raining just enough to make me feel damp and cold."

I stopped and thought about the rain in the woods, how it sounded like fingernails tapping on glass, the drops falling on leaves and timber and broad flat rocks. How it felt like small pieces of the sky falling away from itself.

"Night is coming and I keep running farther and farther into the forest trying to find the voice that is calling out to me, trying to catch up with PeeDee, who is teasing me with this silly game we play. And see, it's different from the swimming pool one because I'm looking for her. She's the Marco and I'm the Polo, but I'm the one who is blind trying to find her, not the other way around.

" 'Marco,' she says, 'Polo,' I say back. And at first it's fun and it's just us messing around. And I'm not afraid or anything because I know I'll find her. We've always played like this so I don't worry or expect anything bad. I just keep running deeper and deeper into these woods calling out the name of some explorer whose life means nothing to me."

I feel Lathin near me.

"Then I don't hear the voice anymore. I don't hear

PeeDee. I keep calling out to her, like we had been in the game, but she doesn't answer. And it gets dark, and suddenly I don't know where I am anymore."

I started to feel afraid, alone, like I do in my dream.

"There's just all these trees and the sounds of the woods and then there's PeeDee's faraway voice again, calling me. First, I don't hear anything and then it's like she's everywhere, in every tree, around every corner calling me. And now she's saying my name, 'Andy, Andy, Andy.' She keeps saying it."

And then I recalled that Lathin didn't know my name up until this point in our conversation. That we never really introduced ourselves; that I had learned his name when the code red was called. And I stopped telling about the dream, because I thought it was odd that after all this time and all this talk, he hadn't asked my name.

"Andreas," I said. "Andy is short for Andreas."

I pulled away from the story for a moment.

"My mother christened me with a lovely name she had heard from California. She didn't know it was a huge crack running through the earth, the fault line where earthquakes are centered."

And this, I remember thinking, was weird, but in that moment, the moment that he heard and learned my name, it seemed as if I felt him reach up and put his hand on the wall behind me, so I waited, but then I turned around in the place I had been sitting, and reached up and put my hand up to the wall too. I stayed there. I pulled the pillow beneath me as I stayed sitting on the floor, facing the wall this time, and then I went on. I kept my hand against his.

"Now it's dark. I walk and I fall. Into trees, on the ground, in thickets and puddles. I fall and I get up and I trip and I fall again. And always, she's calling me. And I can't find her. I can't find anybody. It's just me and the darkness, the chill of night, the marking of time with the light taps of rain, and a little girl's voice calling out my name."

I felt myself start to shake.

"It's the most horrible thing I know."

And that's when I cried. Not real hard at first. But more like I have always cried. Carefully and briefly. Politely, so as not to call attention to myself or create discomfort for those around me.

But somehow, with my hand stretched against the wall, thinking that his hand was there too, a hand that had, just like mine, not reached when it should have reached, not held on or let go or done whatever it was our hands were supposed to have done, I started to feel as if the inside of my soul was peeling away. I clung to the wall like it would save me, like it was holding me up.

It was maybe an hour before dawn, still dark outside, still night.

And in a manner that I have never done before, I wept.

EIGHT

793.3

ANCE

It's funny how passages of time can change how you organize your memories. It's interesting to discover how you decide to share what you share about an important event with other people, how you manage it in your conversations.

Over time, I have learned that I don't always include this particular part of the night when I discuss with family members or close friends what occurred between Lathin and me. It has become a part I do not share.

"Well, what happened next?" my mother has asked more than once after I tell her about the confession and the revelation of my dream.

And on a few separate occasions, when I had a glass of wine or when the night was particularly bright with stars, I have tried to explain to her about what happened last in that night at Holly Pines. I have made an attempt or two to reconstruct the final hour for her.

I once even thought I would tell Charlie because I thought he could understand. I sensed that he wanted to know and that he would let it be held in kindness. However, once I began to tell both Mama and Charlie, once I tried to give an exact account of the final part of our conversation, I found that I wasn't able to.

I stumbled over the memories at first. Then I tried to go back around and pick up what I missed, but I ended up just hurrying through this part, trying to fill in a few minutes of our last hour together. I would stop by saying only that Lathin talked a little about his daughter or that Lathin hummed a song.

Finally, when I am no longer able to come up with any description, I just skip explaining the last hour altogether. I have learned that it simply isn't so easy to put into words what those last minutes of darkness were like. I understand that I cannot say it in a way that makes sense to anybody else.

I am not even fully able to explain what it came to mean to me.

I finish my report by noting that Lathin and I only sat in silence together. I say that neither of us added anything to what had been said. We just rested or waited, I say. We just sat with it, like Quakers in meeting. And that's usually all I tell to anyone who has asked, all I reveal about the night at Holly Pines. That's where I end the events of that evening and move straight to the next morning even though there was something more.

There was something much more.

The new day had not quite yet dawned and there was,

on the night when everything broke open, one more thing that happened between Lathin and me. After a while, a half an hour of silence maybe, I'm not sure about the exact time, Lathin began the final part of our conversation. At the time, it startled me that there was going to be more.

"Mary used to love the rain," he said.

And although by that late hour of our conversation, his voice had become familiar, comforting, I didn't really know where he was going with a line like that.

I felt a bit wrestled from the quiet we had shared, like I needed to clear my head, like I was being awakened from a nap. I listened though. I figured he would get to the right place when he needed to. And, of course, he did.

"From the time she was old enough to walk, she wanted to be in the rain, wanted to stand in it or run through it. She just loved to be outside and get wet."

I noticed how I had grown calm. My breathing slowed down. My pulse seemed steadier. I wasn't even as cold as I had been at an earlier hour in the night.

I turned to see the tree outside, now still and steady after the storm. It was quiet at Holly Pines.

"She had jackets and hats. I made sure she had all that stuff, but she would just run out there with nothing but her clothes."

I remembered being like that as a child. I never minded being caught in a storm. Even as an adult I have never seen much value in umbrellas. I like the feel of rain covering me.

"She'd jump into puddles and dance around like that old white guy who sang that famous song." He stopped.

"What was it called?" he asked.

Before I could answer, he had thought of it.

" 'Singin' in the Rain,' " he said, recalling the tune.

I knew he was talking about Gene Kelly and his well-known version of that old hit. I had seen lots of different dancers and singers do the number, but I knew that his was the most famous.

I thought of a little girl copying his dance steps, twirling her umbrella, gliding about. I recalled doing my own rendition when I was a child probably not much older than his Mary, splashing in the puddles, stepping from the curb to the street, scooping up water with my shoe, gliding along the sidewalks.

"Wouldn't matter where we were, she would drop my hand and leave my side, run to a spot where she stood by herself, way out ahead of me."

He chuckled.

"First couple of times, I worried about her, thought she'd get hit by a car or chased by a dog or something. I'd yell at her to come back."

I figured he should have worried about lightning too, that it was more of a possibility that she would have gotten struck by lightning than bitten by a dog.

"I didn't like her out of a close range. I didn't like not being able to hold her by the hand."

He need not have told me this; I already knew how protective he had been with his little girl.

"But after so many times, I just got used to it. It was what she did, and I understood that it was the one thing I knew she loved more than that game show."

I remembered how earlier in the night he had talked about *The Price Is Right*, how he had mentioned how much she enjoyed that program.

"Mary loved playing in the rain."

I didn't respond. I chose to be quiet and listen, just to let his good memories wash over us both. Besides, it was nice not to have to talk for a little while. I was spent from my own story.

"Once I learned how she liked it, I would watch the weather reports real close every morning and try to figure out how I could get back before the storm started. I wanted to get home as quick as I could so that we could get out there in it."

I heard him take in a big breath. He sounded as content as I felt.

"I'd hurry up the stairs of the apartment building and she would be standing at the door waiting and then she wouldn't even let me inside."

"She pulled me back outside and we would run down the stairs and then she would start."

I waited.

"She'd head out into a big opening somewhere, usually around the parking lot or out in this little place she liked to play." He made a kind of clucking noise.

"She would spread out her arms, stretch out her fingers

while holding them tightly together, making little bowls with her hands, and she would laugh out loud."

I bowed my head. His story just seemed to call for that kind of reverence. I had not heard such a sacred thing since my grandma, just before she died, whispered that she loved me.

"Laugh right out loud," he said again, like this was not his daughter's normal behavior.

I enjoyed the image of a little girl laughing, his little girl laughing. I heard the tenderness in his voice. I knew this was a memory he kept very close to his heart.

"She was catching the tears of God, she'd say."

I tilted my head to listen more closely. It wasn't what I expected to hear.

As if he had seen my surprise, Lathin added, "I know, I never knew where she heard such a thing."

I nodded.

"I had never said anything like that to her about rain and I didn't know anybody around us who had. I figure she just made it up."

He paused.

"I mean, I knew she had heard old folks talk about thunder as God being angry or it being angels who were bowling in Heaven. I knew those old sayings. That wouldn't have surprised me if she had said something like that. I had heard stuff like that before."

So had I.

In the summers, at the farm, Grandma used to say that

thunder was God pacing up in Heaven, throwing things, waiting for the Devil to appear and explain himself for some mischief or trouble he had caused. Then she'd tell us we better hide or that eventually the Lord might grow tired of waiting on Satan and would step down to Earth and take out his anger on us.

I used to believe her and when the clouds would roll in, I used to sit under the kitchen table real quiet, feeling very jittery until the storm passed.

Mama would make me come out when I repeated that kind of behavior at home. She hated all of those things country folks would say. She especially didn't like any talk about God and punishment. I guess she had heard her fair share of that when she was growing up.

I still hid when I was alone in thunder and I was still nervous when she was around and would make me come out. I was always worried that God was out to get me.

"My sister used to say that lightning was God's way of hurling warnings to humans, that it was a sign of what Hell was like and that you better pay attention and move out of the way."

I thought about Lathin's family. I wondered if he ever saw his siblings, if his sister was still afraid of storms.

"But I never heard anybody claiming that rain was the result of God's sadness, that raindrops were tears.

"You ever hear that?" he asked.

I shook my head and then I answered out loud.

"No, I never heard it either," I replied.

"Nah," he responded and then paused, trying to remember anybody ever saying such a thing, I suppose.

"So, that's why I figure she just made it up, pretended, like children will do."

I nodded, thinking he was probably right.

I recalled how during the summers PeeDee and I would make things up about storms and stars. We had theories about everything in nature.

We believed that there was a man in the Moon and that the whole thing was made of cheese. We thought that stars were the lanterns of angels making pilgrimages across the sky.

We decided that snow came from pillow fights in heaven and that wind came from God when He was waving His arms.

Remembering all that PeeDee and I pretended about the weather, it just made sense to me that Mary was the same kind of little girl as we had been.

And then I had another thought. I leaned forward from the wall, even stood up, wondering if I should say it out loud.

I waited.

"Or maybe it was true," I finally said.

"What you mean?" he asked, sounding very interested in what I might suggest.

"Maybe that's what God told her. Maybe that's what rain really is."

I dropped back against the wall considering what I had just said. I didn't know whether I believed that or not, but I figured a little girl would know as well as anybody whether or not God wept and whether or not those tears fell on Earth.

"Well, you could be right," he replied, sounding as if he believed me, as if he thought I just might be telling the truth.

And then, I heard him yawn and I thought that maybe he was going to sleep, that maybe the night was ending. I glanced over to my bed and did think it looked very inviting.

But then he kept talking.

" 'Course, if you are right, then that means God sure does grieve a lot, doesn't it? I mean, looks like every day it's raining somewhere."

I slid back down to my seated position. We were not through yet.

"I guess He has a lot to grieve over," I noted.

"Yeah, I reckon that's about true."

I fluffed up my pillow and repositioned it behind my back. I was starting to feel a little stiff.

"Mary never seemed like it was a sad thing, though," he continued. "Rain always seemed to make her happy, make her want to dance," he added. "It wasn't like she thought of it as grieving."

I considered his observation.

"Maybe she just liked the thought that He grieved," I said.

"What you saying?" he asked.

"I'm saying that maybe Mary liked the thought that God was close enough and involved enough in events and situations on Earth that He felt things, like we do."

I pulled the pillow out and placed it on the floor and lay down again. "There's some peace in that, isn't there?" I asked. "Some comfort?"

"I guess," he replied. "I never put much stock in what God does or doesn't feel," he said. "Never really thought about it one way or the other."

"Me neither," I replied. "But maybe Mary did."

I wondered if such a thing could be true for a child, if such an idea could make a little girl want to play outside in the rain.

"Maybe she liked it because she felt watched over, cared about." I waited and then said, "If I thought that, believed that, I'd probably be out there in the rain too, soaking up the knowledge that I wasn't in this big, cruel world all by myself. Maybe I'd be out there splashing around in it too."

I could feel him smiling at that. And the weird thing was that I believed it. Playing in the rain would be the perfect response to such an action performed by God, such a display of emotion.

"How'd she do it?" I asked, suddenly curious about his little girl's love of rain. "How'd she play in it?"

"She called it dancing," he replied. "Always wanting to go outside in the rain to dance."

"Makes sense," I noted.

"I named it God's Weeping Dance," he said. "Because she always did the same thing."

"Like steps," I said.

"What?"

"Like she had learned dance steps," I replied.

"Oh, right," Lathin responded. "I forgot you knew about that," he added.

"So, tell me about them," I said again.

I'm not sure why I really wanted to know, but I was interested in what his little girl did to celebrate rain, how she looked splashing from puddle to puddle, where he was when he watched and what he was doing.

"Well," he said, recalling the ritual, "at first, she stood perfectly still, like a statue, and then she would tap her feet and raise her hands above her head." He waited a second.

"Then there was the laughing. I already told you about that, but that's what I remember the most."

I nodded, thinking that would be the best memory to keep.

"And then, I would clap for her."

"Like applauding?" I asked, lifting my head up off the pillow.

"No, like a drum," he replied.

I wasn't sure what he meant.

"Along with the rain and the thunder, I gave her the beat," he added.

"Oh," I said, surprised. I hadn't considered his participation in his little girl's play.

"What?" he asked, sounding as if he were making a joke. "You don't think I got rhythm?"

I smiled. "I thought all black people had rhythm."

He snorted at that.

"Yeah, that's true what everybody says, we can all dance

like Michael Jackson and play basketball like Michael Jordan."

I laughed. "What was it like?" I asked.

"What?"

"The beat."

And then, without answering in any words, without talking again, slowly, easily, Lathin explained. He started clapping his hands together.

At first, it was on the first and the third beats in four-four time, and then he switched it up, clapping in surprising places, making an easy, clear cadence. Lightly, with steady time in the background, his foot tapped a strong bass beat.

I leaned against the wall to hear it more clearly. And as he beat out the rhythm, I thought of how it sounded like rain. Like the rain I long for on hot summer days, the rain that wakes me up in the middle of the night.

It was like the rain that promises that everything that was dirty or covered in dust is clean, new, that all of the earth that was parched and dry is now wet with moisture.

It was the sound of a little girl's heartbeat, the cadence of a dream, and as the night made its final pitch before morning, as Lathin beat a rhythm on the floor and on the wall that was between us, I got up from where I was sitting, dropping my covers from around my shoulders, and I began to dance.

I did not worry about someone finding me or seeing me or watching me. I did not think about the consequences of doctors' reports or a nurse's notes written in my chart. I did not think about Calvin or Louise or even the administrator worrying about my cavorting with a known criminal. I did not give one thought to what might happen to me if I was discovered dancing alone in my green cell, just before the light of dawn, when there was no music heard by anyone else but me. But me.

I did not think about what I could not do, how I could not dance. I did not listen to the voice inside my head that demands I look my best or instructs me how to act appropriately. I paid no attention to that tape that plays over and over in my brain, reporting to me the things I should not try.

I did not consider that I was too old to dance the dance of a child or too fat to move and slide across the floor. I did not deliberate as to how I should tap my feet or shake my hips or raise my hands or lift my chin. I did not measure my steps or order my turns.

I did not worry or think or plan or reflect upon anything.

I only danced.

I danced for the child I lost and the child who died. I danced for Mary and her silent tongue and my mother's fear of her own words. I danced for the broken heart and the grief-stricken spirit of my aunt, of a sister, a father, and a girl. I danced for flames that were meant to punish, flowers that never bloomed, and wishes never wished. I danced for restless hands and withered hearts that shrink behind the steel bars of prison.

I danced for my grandfather's malice and his oldest daughter's sorrow, for my father never knowing my name, and for my grandmother carrying the regrets of three generations. I danced for trees that break and splinter from the wind or the weight of little girls, for walls that will not speak, for darkness, for light, and for the places where we hide in fear.

I danced and I danced and I danced.

The night and the tapping and the tears and the things that were lost and found moving in and out of one another, all were a part of the dance that Lathin and I shared together.

It was exactly what it needed to be. It was the loosening of arms and legs and souls. It was the benediction to our night of prayer, a way of sending us both back out into the world. It was the only way of saying amen. And I remember thinking that it was as if I danced myself right into the morning, as if I danced the dawn across the sky and the night with its storm and darkness away. I had danced into a new day.

When I awoke, the sun already high and hot, I was in my bed.

I was in my yellow pajamas looking as if I had been there all night. The sheet and blanket were wrapped around me as if I had been lifted and placed carefully underneath them. All of the linens were neat and ordered as they usually were on my bed.

There was no evidence in the room of all the times I removed the blanket and pillow, threw them on the floor, then replaced them back where they belonged. They were not dirty or soiled. There was no proof of the hours I stood and paced or sat, first in one place, then another. There was no evidence of the fight or the plans or the confession. There was no lingering validation of the dance.

There was nothing out of place. There was no way to demonstrate to myself or to anyone else who might pass by just how long the night had been.

I sat up in the bed and in spite of how things appeared, I remembered. I knew. I turned and glanced around the room. The tree was as it had been before the storm, full and green outside my window. The sun shone brightly through the panes of glass illuminating the green walls around me.

I heard some distant noise, people talking, shouting outside the hallway doors and near the nurses' station. I knew it was morning, a new day, and that the others at Holly Pines were already up and engaged in their scheduled activities. I stayed where I was and listened for a few minutes. I listened to the voices, to the noises around me, the silence close by.

After a bit, I stood up and moved over to where I had been so much of the night.

As I walked over, the chair, I noticed, had been pushed under the desk, perfectly positioned where it should have been. I stood next to the wall. I reached up. It was cold to the touch.

I noticed my watch as I quickly bent down to talk into the vent.

It was well after eight thirty A.M.

NINE

595·7

$\mathcal{B}$UTTERFLIES

"Lathin, Lathin, hey, you awake?"

I heard nothing from next door. There was not one sound. I listened and then dropped to my knees and tapped lightly on the wall.

The hall door opened and closed. I knew that I was supposed to have been dressed and been ready for breakfast more than an hour ago. I stood up just as the door flew open.

"You're sleeping late."

It was Calvin.

He glanced around the room. Just as he had done the night before, he seemed to be studying me and what I may have been doing.

"Yeah," I replied.

Then I yawned and stretched like everything was as it was supposed to be, as if the night had only come and gone like every other night, as if my life were not changed.

"You still working?" I asked him as I looked again at my watch, trying to imagine what Lathin might be doing, wondering if he was still asleep, if he had been given his breakfast, if he was gone.

I was surprised that Calvin was still on duty and wondered if his presence had anything to with the lack of response that I had received from next door.

"It's been a crazy morning," he replied, still looking around. "You've missed a lot of stuff."

"Oh," I said, wondering what kind of stuff he meant.

I thought that the teenager who had been at the end of the hall must have caused more trouble, maybe gotten into a fight with a staff person and ended up having to be restrained. Or, perhaps, I thought, one of the addicts broke into the medicine cabinet and stole a lot of the drugs. I considered the chapel service and thought that maybe Mrs. Naples had gotten filled up with the spirit again.

"You finally get to sleep after your nightmare?" he asked, narrowing his eyes on me.

"Nightmare?" I asked.

Then I immediately recalled what I had told him after he came to my room the second time the previous night. I remembered making up the story so that he would leave me without any suspicion.

"Yes," I answered. "I slept the rest of the night."

"Uh-huh," he said, still studying me, still trying to find something in my story.

I wondered what he knew about me and Lathin and the night we shared and what he thought I would tell him.

"So, Calvin," I asked, moving toward him. "What kind of trouble was at Holly Pines last night?"

"Big trouble," he replied, nodding his head and seeming very serious. It was not how he usually appeared. He was not one who enjoyed drama or liked to spread gossip.

"What's that?" I asked. "What big trouble?"

He walked over to the window and peered out the glass. He seemed to be examining it from end to end. He stood at the left corner and appeared to be looking in the direction of Lathin's room. Then he turned back around to face me.

"There was an escape."

"What? Here?" I asked, shocked that Lathin had done it. And I knew it was Lathin. It had to be Lathin.

"Yeah, here," he said, checking out my reaction.

He waited. "I expect they will want to ask you a few questions about what you know about last night."

"What would I know about last night?" I asked, trying to sound as innocent as I could.

He shrugged. "They'll ask," he said.

"Who's they?" I asked.

"The deputy sheriff," he replied. "The police."

I nodded. I didn't say anything else. I figured it was best just to keep quiet about everything.

Calvin faced the window again and then glanced toward the vent.

I could tell he noticed that the bed was in better shape, different from how it had been in the previous hours he had been in my room. I could see him thinking about things in the room, how they had been, how they were now.

I looked at the furniture as he made a sweeping glance around me. I noticed the bed again, trying to understand how it could have been put in such a right order. I had pulled the linens on and off so many times; there's no way that things could appear as they did the following morning. The entire room was exactly as it should have been, as if nothing out of the ordinary had occurred.

"Get your clothes on. I'll leave the door unlocked. When you're ready, come down to the end of the hall and ring the button. Somebody'll let you out."

Then he turned to walk out my door, stopped, and turned back to face me. "Oh, and by the way, today's your last day. The doctor was here earlier and went through all of your records. He thinks you're ready to go."

Calvin smiled as if he was genuinely happy for me.

I was sure that we both knew it didn't have anything to do with a doctor thinking I was ready to go. We both knew it had to do with the insurance coverage and the fact that I had run out of money.

"I guess you'll need to call somebody to come get you and take you home today."

He waited, dropped his arms at his side. "Who will you call?" he asked.

At first, I thought maybe he was trying to be smart, ask a question to see if I would give him some information about Lathin, about his escape.

I considered that maybe Calvin was suspicious about the two of us working out something together and were planning to meet up somewhere.

I faced the night attendant who had been on duty the entire night and I wondered what he might know, what he might have told anybody, or guessed about Lathin and me. But as I stared at him, I realized that he was harmless. Harmless, I thought, and he had a good heart. Even when I was crazy I could always tell that about people.

"I guess I'll call my mother," I replied, knowing that he didn't suspect a thing. He was asking the question just to make sure I had a ride home.

"I bet she'll be glad to hear from you," he responded.

"I expect she will be," I noted.

Calvin nodded. "Let me know when you're ready to go," he said. And he smiled at me and left the room.

When I heard him walk down the hall, the big door open and close, I waited a few seconds. I stood with my ear pressed against the wall and then I carefully opened my door and walked outside. I made sure that the hall was empty before I made a move to the room at my left and then I quietly headed over to Lathin's door.

I tried to open it but the door was locked. I looked inside the small window. It was bare except for the items that were in every room I had seen at Holly Pines. The furniture was arranged just as it was where I had been staying. Everything appeared neat and sterile.

The bed had been stripped, and I could see the pillowcase down at the foot of it. It was bulky, appeared to be full. I assumed that the other linens were inside it. The desk was cleaned off. The little sink appeared wiped down, and the floor practically shined. There was no sign anywhere that anyone had ever even been in there. There were no pieces of trash around, no papers, no articles of clothing, no handcuffs or chains.

The bars on the window had not been disturbed. The glass was unbroken. And when I looked around to see the vent, the place where he had had sat and shared himself with me, I was shocked. I had expected it to be open or bent in some way. It was perfectly in place.

The vent and the cover were unchanged. Nothing was out of the ordinary or looked as if it had been vandalized or altered or even used in any way. I couldn't believe everything in the room was so undisturbed. I placed my hand on the door, then on the window, and didn't even feel as if his presence had been there; and for a moment, I actually had to convince myself that he had really been next door only a few hours before.

I examined his room from end to end, ceiling to floor, wall to wall. If Lathin had escaped, I don't know how he did it. I don't know how he fixed everything to be so clean and neat. I don't know how he could have left and not made any noise to wake me or give any clue that he was doing what he apparently did. I do not know what possibly could have happened in the couple of hours between my falling to sleep and when I awoke.

I stood at his door and considered all of the possibilities. I imagined that he could have snuck out of the door and down the hall, perhaps even sliding by the nurses' station without being noticed. And yet, even if he had been able to get that far, then there were all of the locks and alarms. I couldn't figure out how he could have managed getting through all of those.

I remembered how he had said that going through the window was his best option, but as I examined the opening on the far wall of the room, away from the door, I could not envision a man as big as he sliding through it. And even if he could sneak out, I had to wonder, how did the glass not break? How did the bars not get pulled out or broken?

I stared into the room in which he had stayed and considered what could have happened. And as I wondered about Lathin and his escape, I became worried that he had been caught. I became concerned that someone had discovered him leaving the facility or the grounds and that at some time in the previous hours of that early morning, Lathin had been captured and sent back to prison, or worse, killed in his attempt. And since I was not supposed to know that he was even there, I didn't know how or who to ask about him.

I left his door and went back to my room. I sat on my bed and thought about what Calvin had said, that I was wanted for questioning. I realized that I was going to be asked about the night and if I had any knowledge about anything odd or strange that occurred in the room next to mine.

I sat and considered my answers, the story I would give to the officials, and then I also remembered that Calvin said I was discharged, that I was going home. I was hopeful that I could leave before anyone thought to stop me to ask me any questions. I stood up and changed out of my pajamas into my jeans and a shirt. I gathered up my belongings.

I packed up my clothes and bagged the few things they

let me keep during my stay at Holly Pines, my toothbrush, my comb, my lotion. When I walked over to the desk and opened the drawer, I saw my journal, placed neatly inside. And that was when I noticed my pen, the one I had thrown to Lathin through the vent earlier in the night, the one that he had said did not make it to him, the one he had said to leave alone and not try to recover.

I took it out and examined it, trying to find something that might tell me more about what had happened with Lathin. I couldn't imagine how it had gotten back into my room, how Lathin could have gotten out of his chains or handcuffs—whatever it was that bound him—unlocked his door and then mine and walked into my room without me hearing a thing, without anybody hearing a thing.

I searched, but the pen told no story. There were no marks or scratches on it, nothing missing from it. It even still wrote just as it had in the previous days. It appeared as if it had not been used for anything but writing. As I held it in my hand, turning it over and over, studying it, scrutinizing it, it became very clear to me that sometime in that morning, sometime during that very brief period when I slept, Lathin had been there, in my room, near my bed, near me.

Sometime late in the night, just as dawn approached, Lathin had managed to get out of his handcuffs or chains, get out of his room and come into mine. And that sometime in the dark hours of this new day, Lathin had said good-bye to me and run away. I realized that this man, this prison inmate, this stranger, this friend, had been close enough to touch me and I had not known it.

I put the pen and the journal into my suitcase, set it by the closet, and finished preparing myself to leave Holly Pines. I packed everything I had brought with me. I walked over to the wall and placed my hand upon it. I closed my eyes and remembered all that we had shared, all that we had confessed. I took a deep breath and headed out the door and down the hall.

I met with the charge nurse, a new person who was filling in while the normal staff was being interrogated about the events of the weekend. Her name was Dotty and I considered saying something about how odd it was for a woman with her name to be working in a psychiatric hospital, but I decided I should try and maintain a low profile. I didn't want her figuring out who I was and calling over the deputy. I was polite and did only what was instructed.

She asked me a lot of questions, all written on a form that she placed on a clipboard and read off to me. They mostly were geared to help me articulate how it was that I planned to move back into my life, how I saw myself returning to life beyond the walls of Holly Pines.

I answered her as succinctly and clearly as I was able. I planned to return to my job at the library, planned to live in my same apartment, planned to keep a regular appointment with a therapist in town. And as I answered the discharge questions, I realized that I really was ready to go, I really was better than I had been when I answered the questions asked of me during my admittance.

I signed the form and was allowed to call my mother. She picked up on the third ring and after crying a bit, she

promised to pick me up by lunchtime. I placed my belongings in a storage room near the nurses' station and was allowed to go to breakfast.

While I was in the cafeteria, I saw the deputy sheriff talking to the nurses, the doctor who had been on call, and
Calvin. I could feel that Calvin was watching me, and even
though I prepared myself, neither the deputy nor anyone
else ever came over to ask me any questions.

Later, just before my mother arrived and just as Calvin
was trying to leave, I watched as he was getting ready to de-
part. I decided to follow him and ask what had happened, if
they had captured Lathin, if he had gotten away, if he had
been shot. I stopped him just as he was heading out the rear
door, the one the staff used to come and go from the facility.
Patients weren't allowed where I had gone, but I thought I'd
have a little leeway since I was officially checked out of Holly
Pines.

He didn't hear me walk up behind him.

"Hey," I said softly, trying not to startle him.

"Oh, hey," he said. He was taking off his badge and placing it in the backpack I had always seen him carrying.

"Long night, I guess," I said, stepping around to face
him.

"Yep," he replied. "I hope everything goes well for you
at home," he said, sounding very sincere.

"Thanks, Calvin, for you too," I replied, thinking that
sounded very stupid of me to say.

He nodded and looked as if he was anxious to leave. He
ran his hands through his hair. He was tired.

"Calvin," I said quietly. "Was it Lathin who escaped? Was it the prisoner?"

He looked me straight in the eyes and I realized then that he knew that something had happened in the two rooms at the end of the hall. It was clear that he had suspected that something had transpired between the two of us.

"Now, Andy, you know there aren't any prisoners at Holly Pines."

I thought I saw a slight smile. He continued, "There isn't any patient here by that name." He almost sounded convincing.

He winked and moved around me, heading out the door and to the parking lot. And that had been all that I ever heard from anyone at Holly Pines about the man or the escape or even the night itself.

The deputy and a few state police officers who came and went in and out of the psychiatric facility never questioned me, never even seemed to know who I was. It was as if they never even saw me. No nurse or doctor called me out or searched me or my belongings. Calvin had not told anyone what he had seen or heard or even thought about the two inpatients at the end of the hall. As if he had somehow understood the sacredness of what had happened, the night attendant did not share anything with anyone.

I sat in the waiting area and observed as the investigators walked past me two or three times acting very perturbed and excited. I watched them take calls on their cell phones and talk in code about what had happened. The entire time they never even noticed me, never looked at me as if I had any information that might be helpful in their search. And I never let on any differently.

Months later when I finally spoke of it, Charlie said that maybe it was all just a dream or some transcendental experience. He suggested that maybe there really never was any person named Lathin Hawkins, since the administration to this day still makes that claim. He says that maybe the twenty-eight days and the sessions with the doctors and the group meetings, the time I spent with the counselors, dislodged the memory about PeeDee and once that happened, it just all came loose during that final night I was there. He had read about this very thing, he told me. Breakthroughs come by a variety of means, he noted.

I just smiled and nodded.

Mama had another idea. After she picked me up that morning—holding me tighter than she needed to, saying that God had finally answered her prayers and that I would be okay—I told her about Lathin.

I told her about what had happened that night, how he had gotten me to talk about PeeDee, a name she and I hadn't spoken since the accident. I told her that we had stayed up all night and talked and that it was the key that unlocked my heart and then I told her about the escape and how no one confirmed that he had even been there.

Mama listened intently at my story and then responded that it had been a miracle, that Lathin had been a messenger sent by God. After she explained that she had found religion while I was locked up, that in my time at the hospital she had taken to reading the Bible, she decided that the whole event was of a completely spiritual nature.

She said that Lathin was some celestial being wrestling with me all night just like the story of Jacob from the Old Testament, that I didn't let him go until I got my blessing. And then she kept talking and got that story mixed up with some movie she had seen and said that God had heard my prayers and sent me a guardian angel like the one in that film that plays every Christmas with James Stewart.

She decided that my spiritual attendant hadn't been a clumsy rookie like the overwrought heavenly herald to the distressed banker in the movie, but rather one disguised as a prison inmate. And she said that he had helped me see what I had needed to see and that when his work was done, he just disappeared into the night.

Later, Mama asked me if I had heard anything that morning, a bell ring or a chime. I shook my head.

"There were no bells," I reported.

When I ask them both, however, the obvious questions, about who escaped, why the deputy sheriff was there, and why Calvin had winked at me like he knew, they just shrug their shoulders like they don't have to know all the answers for their idea to be right. They both seem to prefer the mysterious to the probable and like thinking they know best.

The truth is, there are probably a lot of possible scenarios that folks could say about what happened at Holly Pines, about Lathin and his disappearance. I'm sure that there would be lots of speculations about the event. But I don't know them all since it isn't something I talk about that often anyway. It's not a night I recount to very many people.

I just keep it to myself and remember it the same way I remember how Charlie looked when he invited me out the following autumn to a college homecoming party, like we were coeds or something. How he wouldn't look in my eyes, like he was afraid to ask, all flushed and vulnerable. How he seemed to think I'd say no and then how he smiled only a little when I said, "Of course." The way I instantly loved him for knowing how much I wanted to dance.

I keep the thoughts I have about that night and what I shared with Lathin the same way I keep the feelings I had when I first realized I was pregnant with my and Charlie's first child. The life that I knew was growing inside me, that was me but not me.

The way my mother reached for my hand on the day we learned that Aunt LuEller had died.

I have learned in a real way, a deep way, that there are some things that can't be ordered and talked about because they go deeper than just how we gather up information and explain things, the way we sum up our lives at cocktail parties in a manner that can be appreciated by acquaintances.

I know that Lathin Hawkins was real because I was there. I was with him. And I am better because of him. I know that the stories I remember about myself and about him that we told through a vent that stretched between us are true because we told them from our hearts.

I know that the night is as I recall it and that the tears and the memories and the music he played on the wall that separated us, on the floor beneath him, unbound me and set me free.

I know it. I believe it. I am changed because of it. And nothing anybody says to try and organize the night, categorize the night, make sense of the night is going to cause it to be different in my mind or in my heart. I left Holly Pines and because of what happened between me and Lathin, began my life again.

The fall after that dry summer I started taking classes at the college. At first, it was just a course here and there, the basic requirements for any liberal arts degree. I took science and math and English and psychology. And then I knew what I really wanted to study. It was as clear as falling in love.

In spite of how I felt about it, my resolve to follow my passion, it was, however, not so well received. It was quite a shock to a lot of people including Charlie, my mother, and the head of the department, when I, well past the age of thirty, declared dance as my major. There were a few meetings in which I was asked a number of times if this was really what I wanted. I never wavered in my decision.

I admit that I was never much of a performer. The classes were quite difficult for me and I certainly had the least talent of any of the dance students. They were all so young and graceful and lovely and all members of some dance company or had regular concerts or recitals. I, however, danced just one time in a public. Performing in a concert was a requirement for the major and I finally had to participate in my senior year. I was as nervous as I've ever been about anything, but I did it. I put on my leotard and brightly covered scarves, held my head high, and I did it. I danced on a stage in front of more than a hundred people.

I called my piece "The Butterfly's Return," and I used the music of West African drums. It was only three and a half minutes long, but it was everything I had. It was critiqued by my professor as "primitive, haunting, and telling a story that can only be moved," and I was delighted because I thought she absolutely understood what I had done.

I graduated in four years and discovered I have a very good eye for choreography and lighting design. I lit most of the stages for the recitals of fellow students, did a lot of the choreography while I was in school. They were always asking for my help and I liked doing the shows. It's been said, in fact, that I "can light a stage and choreograph a performance to appear as if the audience has left their seats and entered into the soul of the dancers."

My first piece was danced by a young friend of mine who was tall and carried the same long lines I remember from Miss LaVelle's arms and legs and was dedicated to Lathin. It was entitled, "The Dance of the Weeping God" and was showcased all around the state, and I often wondered if he ever heard of it or if he ever even thought again of me.

Of course, I like to think he got away and that he's living somewhere in a peaceful place where he is able to find some darkness, feel relieved from the light. I like to think he is no longer alone or angry or chained behind any bars and that he's happy, finding reason to laugh at rain or clap himself a nice rhythm. I like to think of him as free.

Funny thing, when Mama came to get me from Holly Pines that day of my release, she said she drove around a bit in the town of Vanceboro because she got lost. She said that as she made her way down one of the main streets, she had seen a young woman, her skin the color of dark honey with her face holding the kindest smile Mama had ever seen, standing on a corner looking like she was waiting for someone.

My mother pulled over to ask her if she knew where the psychiatric hospital was, and that this woman, in her thirties maybe, beautiful she said, dressed in a long lavender dress with the tiniest white flowers and tied with a purple satin bow, had just looked at her and laughed out loud.

"Just laughed out loud," Mama repeated. "Like she knew a secret about the place or something."

And that's how I like to think about him.

That he had found a way to get loose, to get free. And that Mary had met him on that bright hot morning somewhere on a street corner not far from the hospital with the means to take him away. And that now he is just as he dreamed he would be, in a city someplace that does not know him or his crime, walking in the rain, laughing, clapping his hands for his risen, dancing daughter.

And that, I think, is as it should be.

Nothing askew or out of place. Nothing broken or hidden or politely kept from view. The living of a life. The dance of confession and absolution. A friendship breaking through walls.

The lovely and complete, the perfect order of things.